Untie this sack of stories and you will find . . . a Martian wearing Granny's jumper, a mongoose, a unicorn, a princess who is a pig, that well-known comic fairy-tale pair Handsel and Gristle and many other strange and exciting characters.

No story has been put in the sack without very careful inspection by children's book specialist Pat Thomson. All the stories are tried and tested favourites, and all by top children's authors – Penelope Lively, Michael Rosen, Terry Jones, Joan Aiken, Peter Dickinson and many others.

You won't want to stop reading until you get right to the bottom of the sack!

PAT THOMSON is a well-known author and anthologist. Additionally, she works as a lecturer and librarian in a teacher training college – work which involves a constant search for short stories which have both quality and child-appeal. She is also an Honorary Vice-President of the Federation of Children's Book Groups. She is married with two grown-up children and lives in Northamptonshire.

D0453194

Also available by Pat Thomson,
and published by Doubleday and Corgi Books:

A POCKETFUL OF STORIES FOR
FIVE YEAR OLDS

A BUCKETFUL OF STORIES FOR
SIX YEAR OLDS

A BASKET OF STORIES FOR
SEVEN YEAR OLDS

A CHEST OF STORIES FOR
NINE YEAR OLDS

A SATCHEL OF SCHOOL STORIES

A STOCKING FULL OF
CHRISTMAS STORIES

A
SACKFUL
of Stories for
Eight Year Olds

COLLECTED BY PAT THOMSON

Illustrated by Paddy Mounter

CORGI BOOKS

A SACKFUL OF STORIES FOR EIGHT YEAR OLDS
A CORGI BOOK 0 552 527300

First published in Great Britain by Doubleday, a division of Transworld
Publishers Ltd.

PRINTING HISTORY
Doubleday edition published 1990
Corgi edition published 1992
Corgi edition reprinted 1993 (twice)

Collection copyright © 1990 by Pat Thomson
Illustrations copyright © 1990 by Paddy Mounter

The right of Pat Thomson to be identified as the Author of this work has
been asserted in accordance with the Copyright, Designs and Patents Act
1988.

Conditions of sale

1. This book is sold subject to the condition that it shall not, by way of
trade or otherwise, be lent, re-sold, hired out or otherwise circulated
without the publisher's prior consent in any form of binding or cover
other than that in which it is published and without a similar condition
including this condition being imposed on the subsequent purchaser.

2. This book is sold subject to the Standard Conditions of Sale of Net
Books and may not be re-sold in the UK below the net price fixed by the
publishers for the book.

Corgi Books are published by Transworld Publishers Ltd, 61–63
Uxbridge Road, Ealing, London W5 5SA, in Australia by Transworld
Publishers (Australia) Pty. Ltd, 15–25 Helles Avenue, Moorebank, NSW
2170, and in New Zealand by Transworld Publishers (N.Z.) Ltd,
3 William Pickering Drive, Albany, Auckland.

Printed and bound in Great Britain by Cox & Wyman Ltd,
Reading, Berks.

Acknowledgements

The editor and publisher are grateful for permission to include the following copyright stories.

Joan Aiken, 'The Gift Pig' from *A Harp of Fishbones* (Cape, 1972) by Joan Aiken. Reprinted by permission of the author.

Ruth Ainsworth, 'The Flood' from *The Ten Tales of Shellover* (1963). Reprinted by permission of André Deutsch Ltd.

Peter Dickinson, 'Unicorn' from *Merlin Dreams* (1988). Reprinted by permission of Victor Gollancz Limited.

Winifred Finlay, 'The Seal and the Man of Shetland', from *Folk Tales From Moor and Mountain* (Kaye & Ward, 1969), copyright © Winifred Finlay 1969. Reprinted by permission of Dr E. Finlay.

Terry Jones, 'Tim O'Leary' from *Fairy Tales* by Terry Jones. Reprinted by permission of Pavilion Books.

Sheila Lavelle, 'The Cheeseburger', Chapter Four from *Trouble With The Fiend* by Sheila Lavelle, copyright © Sheila Lavelle 1984. Reprinted by permission of Hamish Hamilton Limited.

Penelope Lively, 'A Martian Comes to Stay' from *Uninvited Ghosts* (Heinemann, 1984), copyright © Penelope Lively 1974, 1977, 1981, 1984.

Ruth Michaelis-Jena, 'The Three Sisters' by Ruth Michaelis-Jena. Reprinted by permission of Canongate Publishing.

Philippa Pearce, 'The Manatee' from *Lion at School and Other Stories*, copyright © Philippa Pearce 1985 (Viking Kestrel, 1985). Reprinted by permission of Penguin Books Limited.

Michael Rosen, 'Handsel and Gristle' from *Hairy Tales and Nursery Crimes* (1985). Reprinted by permission of André Deutsch Limited.

Rosemary Sutcliff, 'Persephone' from *The Faber Book of Greek Legends*, ed. Kathleen Lines (1973), copyright © Rosemary Sutcliff 1973. Reprinted by permission of Murray Pollinger, Literary Agent.

CONTENTS

A SACKFUL OF STORIES
FOR EIGHT YEAR OLDS

A Martian Comes to Stay

It was on the second day of Peter's holiday with his grandmother that the Martian came to the cottage. There was a knock at the door and when he went to open it there was this small green person with webbed feet and eyes on the end of stumpy antennae who said, perfectly politely, 'I wonder if I might bother you for the loan of a spanner?'

'Sure,' said Peter. 'I'll ask my gran.'

Gran was in the back garden, it being a nice sunny day. Peter said, 'There's a Martian at the door who'd like to borrow a spanner.'

Gran looked at him over her knitting. 'Is there, dear? Have a look in Grandad's toolbox, there should be one there.'

That's not what your grandmother would have said? No, nor mine either but Peter's gran was an unusual lady, as you will discover.

1

Grandad had died a few years earlier and she lived alone in this isolated cottage in the country, growing vegetables and keeping chickens, and Peter liked going to stay with her more than almost anything he could think of. Gran was not like most people. She was unflappable and what you might call open-minded, which accounts for everything that happened next.

Peter found the spanner and took it back to the Martian, who held out a rather oddly constructed hand and thanked him warmly. 'We've got some trouble with the gears or something and had to make an emergency landing. And now the mechanic says he left his tools back at base. I ask you! It's all a mystery to me – I'm just the steward. Anyway – thanks a lot. I'll bring it back in a minute.' And he padded away up the lane. There was no one around, but then there wasn't likely to be: the cottage was a quarter of a mile from the village and hardly anyone came by except the occasional farm tractor and the odd holidaymaker who'd got lost. Peter went back into the garden.

'Should have offered him a cup of tea,' said Gran. 'He'll have had a fair journey, I shouldn't wonder.'

'Yes,' said Peter. 'I didn't think of that.'

2

In precisely three minutes time there was a knock at the door. The Martian was there, looking distinctly agitated. He said, 'They've gone.'

'Who's gone?' said Peter.

'The others. The spaceship. All of them. They've taken off and left me.'

Gran, by now, had come through from the garden. She hitched her specs up her nose and looked down at the Martian, who was about three and a half feet high. 'You'd best come in,' she said, 'while we have a think. Gone, you say? Where was it, this thing of yours?'

'Over there,' said the Martian, pointing across the lane.

'Ah,' said Gran. 'Ted Thomas's field.'

'The one with the bullocks in,' added Peter.

'Bullocks?' said the Martian.

'Big brown animals,' explained Peter.

'Animals?' said the Martian.

'Creatures that walk about and eat, like you and me, only different.'

The Martian nodded. 'I saw them, then. I hoped they were harmless.'

'They are,' said Peter.

'But curious,' said Gran. 'They'd have wanted to have a look at this space whatsit, wouldn't they? Stand round it in a circle, making heavy breathing noises. Would they be a bit jumpy, your friends, Mr er . . . ?'

'Very,' said the Martian. 'We tend to be, when we get off-course. I'm dead jumpy right now. For one thing, I'm frightened of that thing in the corner that makes a ticking noise. Is it going to blow up?'

Peter explained about clocks.

Gran, meanwhile, had put the kettle on. 'The way I see it, these friends of Mr, er . . . looked out and saw Ted's bullocks and lost their heads, and who's to blame them? Still, it's not very nice, leaving him stuck here like this. I mean, it's not as though we can give the village taxi a ring and get him home like that. I don't know what's to be done for the best, I really don't. Meanwhile, we'll have a nice cup of tea.'

Tea and a couple of digestive biscuits cheered the Martian up. He sat on the footstool by the stove and apologized for being such a nuisance. 'Not at all,' said Gran. 'We don't get a lot of company round here. It's you I'm bothered about. But anyway, we've got the attic room empty so you're welcome to stop until we can work something out. You'll be company for Peter.' She gazed for a moment at the visitor

4

and went on, delicately, 'Are you, er, young or old, as you might say?'

'I'm three hundred and twenty-seven,' said the Martian.

'Ah,' said Gran. 'Then there's a bit of an age-gap, on the face of it. Peter's nine. Still, it's the spirit that counts, isn't it? That's what I always find, anyway.'

The Martian was an adaptable visitor. He felt the cold rather and preferred to sit right up against the stove and once, with further apologies, got into the oven for a bit to warm

5

up. 'Get a lot of sun, do you, where you come from?' asked Gran. But the Martian was rather vague about his home surroundings; it was different, he said – adding hastily that of course he didn't mean it was better. Once or twice he looked out of the window a trifle nervously. He wanted to know why the trees kept moving.

'It's the wind, dear,' said Gran, who tended to take people into the family once she liked them.

'They're not aggressive?'

'Not to speak of.'

Later, they watched television. The Martian was interested but inclined to raise questions. 'Is it true to life?' he enquired, in the middle of *Top of the Pops*.

'No,' said Peter. 'At least not most people's.'

'What about this?' asked the Martian presently, when *Dallas* was on.

'I wouldn't say so,' said Gran. 'But then I've had a limited experience.'

He appreciated *Zoo Quest*, which was about South American creatures. 'That's Nature,' said Gran. 'It's very highly thought of nowadays. Time I got us something to eat.' She looked doubtfully at the Martian. 'You're not on a

6

special diet or anything like that, I hope?'

But the Martian proved admirably easy to feed. He was a bit wary of sausages but discovered a passion for jam tarts. 'You tuck in,' said Gran. 'You'll be hungry, after that journey.'

Over the next couple of days he settled in nicely. He insisted on helping with the washing-up and played Monopoly with Peter. Peter won every time, which he found embarrassing. The Martian didn't seem to grasp the idea of making money. 'Why do I want to have more and more of these bits of paper?'

'So that you can buy things,' Peter explained.

'Things to eat?'

'Well, no. It's streets and hotels and things, in the game.'

'Mind,' said Gran, 'he's got a point. It's something I've wondered about myself. Maybe you should try a game of cards.'

They played Snap and Rummy but this wasn't much better. The Martian preferred not to win.

'To my mind,' said Gran, 'they've got a different outlook on life, wherever he comes from.' She was knitting the Martian a sweater now. 'Would you come here a minute, dear, just so I can measure it across the chest.' The

7

Martian stood in front of her obligingly. Gran stretched the knitting across his greenish, rather leathery body. 'It's to keep the chill out,' she went on. 'Being as you feel the cold so. I've no objection at all to a person going around in the altogether if that's what they're used to, let's get that clear. There – that's a nice fit.'

The Martian was quite embarrassingly grateful.

He did not venture outside, which seemed on the whole advisable in any case. Neighbours, in remote country districts, tend to be inquisitive about other people's visitors and the Martian would be an odd one to have to explain. 'I suppose,' said Peter, 'we could say he's a distant relative who's come from somewhere abroad.'

'That's not going to satisfy some folks I could name,' said Gran. 'Not with him being as unusual-looking as he is. Even if we said he took after another branch of the family. No, it's best if he stays put till his friends come back. D'you think they'll take long, dear?'

The Martian shook his head doubtfully. He said he thought they would come, eventually, but that they might be having difficulty finding the right spot again. 'Well, not to worry,' said

Gran. 'We'll just bide our time till they do.'

After several days the Martian overcame his worries about trees and various noises that bothered him such as birds and dogs barking, and sat in a deckchair in the garden, wearing Gran's sweater and with a rug round him. On one of these occasions old Mr Briggs from down the lane came past with his dog and stopped for a moment to chat to Gran over the wall. 'Ah,' he said, glancing over her shoulder. 'Got another of your grandchildren stopping with you, then?'

'In a manner of speaking,' said Gran evasively.

Mr Briggs departed, calling over his shoulder, 'See you at the village fête, Saturday.'

Gran sat down again. 'It's a shame we can't take him along to the fête. Be ever so interesting for him. I mean, it's what you want, when you're in foreign parts – have a look at how other people set about things. The Flower Show'll be a treat this year, with the good weather we've been having.'

The Martian said wistfully that he'd love to go.

'I wonder,' said Gran. 'Let's see now. S'pose we . . . '

And then Peter had a brilliant idea. In the cupboard under the stairs there was an old pushchair that had been used for him and his sister when they were small. If they put the Martian in that and covered him up with a pram-rug and put something round his head, he could pass for a small child. Gran clapped her hands. 'Clever boy! There now, we'll have ourselves an outing!' The Martian beamed, if someone with antennae, a mouth somewhat like a letter-box and not much else by way of features can be said to beam.

'You know,' Gran confided to Peter later on, when they were alone, 'I've really took to him. You can tell he's been brought up nicely, from his manners. There's some human beings I know would be put to shame.'

The day of the fête was fine and dry. The Martian was installed in the pushchair, swathed in a blue rug that Gran had crocheted a long time ago and with an old pixie hood that had belonged to Peter's sister on his head. His antennae poked out through two holes, which did not look quite right, so they had to fix a sunshade to the handles of the pushchair and drape some muslin over this; in this way the Martian was only dimly visible as a muffled form. 'We'll say he's sensitive to sunstroke,' said Gran, 'if anyone gets nosy.' They set off for the village with Peter in charge of the pushchair.

The Martian was fascinated with everything he saw. He asked them to stop for him to admire the Amoco Garage with its swags of flapping plastic flags and brightly coloured signs about Four Star Petrol and Credit Cards Accepted. He found it, he declared, very beautiful.

'Well,' said Gran doubtfully, 'to my mind that's on the garish side, but I suppose it's a matter of taste.' The Martian said humbly that he probably hadn't been here long enough yet to be much of a judge of these things. He gazed at the display of baked beans tins and cornflakes packets in the window of the Minimarket and asked anxiously if that would be considered handsome. 'Not really,' said Peter. 'I mean, it's the sort of thing that's so ordinary you don't really notice.'

'He's seeing a different angle to us,' said Gran. 'Stands to reason, when you think about it.'

The smell of petrol made him sneeze. Mrs Lilly from the Post Office, who happened to be passing at the time, craned her head round to stare into the pushchair. 'Bless its little heart, then! Tishoo! She bent down. 'Little boy or a little girl, is it?'

'Boy,' said Gran. 'I wouldn't be surprised if that cold wasn't giving way to something worse,' she added loudly. Mrs Lilly backed away.

They reached the village green, on which the fête was taking place. The band was already playing. The Martian peered out from under the sunshade. 'Watch it!' said Peter warningly. 'People'll see you.' The Martian apologized. 'It's just that it's all so exciting.'

'We always put on a good show,' said Gran modestly. 'It's a question of upstaging Great Snoggington down the road, up to a point,' she explained. The Martian, under the sunshade, nodded. Gran pointed out the Vicar and the head teacher from the village school and Mr Soper who ran the pub. 'They are your leaders?' asked the Martian.

'In a manner of speaking,' said Gran.

They toured the Bring and Buy stall and the Flower Tent. Gran paused to cast a professional eye over the sweet peas. Peter took out his money to see if he had enough left for another ice-cream. Neither of them saw Susie Stubbs, who was aged three and in Peter's opinion the most appalling brat in the village, sidle up to the pushchair. She put out a fat finger and poked the Martian, who sat perfectly still. Susie stuck her face under the sunshade.

There was an earsplitting shriek. Susie's mum, busy in the middle of a piece of juicy gossip with a friend, broke off and came rushing over.

'Ooooh . . . !' wailed Susie. 'An 'orrible fing! An 'orrible fing like a snail! Oooh – I don't like it! Want to go home! Want my mum! Take it away! Ooh, an 'orrible fing in that pram!'

'There, my pet,' cooed Susie's mum. 'There, there . . . Did she have a nasty fright, then? Let's buy her an iced lolly, shall we?'

''Orrible fing . . . ' howled Susie, pointing at the pushchair.

Gran glared. She jerked the pushchair away, nearly dislodging the Martian.

'There now, my duckie,' said Susie's mum. 'Why don't you ask the little girl if she'd like to come and play, then?'

'Boy,' snapped Gran. 'Pity he's got such a shocking case of chicken-pox or he'd have liked to, wouldn't you then, Johnnie? 'Bye now, Mrs Stubbs.'

An interested group of observers had gathered. Peter and Gran departed hastily. 'Sorry

about that,' said Gran to the Martian. The Martian replied politely that where he came from also young people were sometimes inclined to be tiresome.

They left the Flower Tent, pausing for Gran to have a word with one or two friends. Curiosity, though, had now been aroused; people kept casting interested glances at the pushchair. 'That your Ron's youngest?' enquired Mrs Binns from the shop. 'Eh?' said Gran loudly; she was expert at producing sudden onsets of deafness when convenient.

Outside, they sat down to watch the police dog display. One of the dogs, which was supposed to be tracking a man who was supposed to be an escaped criminal, kept rushing over and sniffing at the pushchair. 'Get away, you brute,' snarled Gran. The Martian, beneath the sunshade, kept bravely silent but had turned quite pale when Peter took a look at him. He fetched some orange juice from the Refreshment Tent. 'Thank you,' said the Martian faintly.

A stout figure swathed in several Indian bedspreads sat under a sign which declared her to be MADAME RITA, THE INTERNATIONALLY FAMOUS PALMIST AND FORTUNE-TELLER. 'That's the Vicar's wife,' said Gran. 'I'm not having her nosing around my future.' Nevertheless, she veered in that direction. The Vicar's wife, her face blotted out by an enormous pair of sunglasses, seized Gran's hand and predicted a tall dark stranger next Thursday. 'That'll be him that comes to read the meter,' said Gran. 'Well-built, I'd call him, rather than tall, but never mind.'

The Vicar's wife, bending down, lifted the muslin draped over the Martian's sunshade. 'What about the baby, then – let's have your hand, duckie.' She gave a gasp of horror. 'Oh, my goodness, the poor little dear, what-ever . . . '

'Whatever what?' said Gran frostily.

The Vicar's wife dropped the muslin. 'Well, he's a nice little thing, of course, but . . . well . . . unusual.'

Gran gave her a withering look. 'I'd say those specs you've got on aren't doing you any good, Mrs Mervyn. Fashionable they may be but not what I'd call serviceable. Well, I'd best be getting on.'

'Whew!' said Peter, when they were out of earshot. 'It's getting a bit dodgy here.'

Gran agreed. 'Anyway, he's seen a bit of our way of life, that's the main thing. We'll get home now.'

But the damage had been done. There was gossip. The village had been alerted. The next day, three people turned up at the cottage declaring that they happened to be passing and hadn't seen Gran for a month of Sundays and had been wondering how she was. Gran managed to get rid of them all. The Martian sat by the stove saying sadly that he was afraid he was becoming a problem. 'It's not you that's the problem,' said Gran. 'It's human nature.'

All the same, they realized that he could not stay there for ever. 'At least, not without us becoming world famous,' said Peter. 'And him being put on the telly and that kind of thing.'

'I shouldn't care for that,' said the Martian in alarm. 'I'm basically very shy.'

They discussed what was to be done. The Martian said he thought that probably his companions would be trying to find the spot at which they had landed but were having navigational problems.

'Anything you can think of we could do to lend a hand?' enquired Gran.

'We could signal,' said Peter. 'In their language. He could tell us what to say.'

The Martian became quite excited. He'd need some kind of radio transmitter, he said.

17

Gran shook her head. 'I've not got one of those to hand. But there's Jim's big torch up in the attic. We could flash that, like, when it's dark.'

They had their first signal session that evening. The Martian dictated a series of long and short flashes and Peter and Gran took it in turns to stand at the window with the lights off, waving the torch at the sky. Gran thoroughly enjoyed it. She wanted to put in all sorts of extras like invitations to tea and enquiries about whether they preferred fruit cake or a nice jam sponge. She hoped there wouldn't be misunderstandings. 'We don't want one of them satellites coming down in Ted Thomas's field. Or a bunch of them RAF blokes.'

But nothing happened. They decided to try again the next night.

They had been at it for an hour or two – with a break to watch *Coronation Street*, to which the Martian was becoming dangerously addicted – when there was a knock at the door.

'Oh, it's you, Bert,' said Gran. 'What's up, then? Don't you start telling me I've got no telly licence, because I have. Top drawer of the dresser, have a look for yourself.'

The village policeman was standing there.

He said heavily, 'I'm obliged to ask you if I might come in and look round the premises, Mrs Tranter.'

'What's all this posh talk for?' said Gran. 'Come on in. Help yourself.' She put the torch on the table.

The policeman eyed it. 'Would you mind telling me what you've been employing that for the use of, Mrs Tranter?'

'That,' snapped Gran, 'is a torch, and if you don't know what torches are for, Bert Davies, then you'll never make sergeant, frankly.'

The policeman, a little red now around the neck, met Gran's glare valiantly, eyeball to eyeball. 'Would you by any chance, Mrs Tranter, have been passing information to a foreign power?'

There was an awful silence, Peter and the Martian, who was cowering behind the stove, exchanged nervous glances.

'Bert Davies,' said Gran at last, 'I've known you since you was in nappies. You come here asking that kind of thing once more – just once more – and I'm off down the village to have a word with your mum.' She glared at the policeman, who was now a rich strawberry colour to the roots of his hair, and was backing towards the door.

'There's been reports,' he said. 'Reports about flashing lights and that. It's my duty to investigate.'

'It's your duty to get back to the village and see about them motorbike boys that's always charging through over the speed limit,' snapped Gran.

It was at that moment that Peter heard a curious whirring noise from somewhere outside. The policeman, mercifully, was too unnerved to pay any attention, if indeed he heard anything; he retreated to his car, with as much dignity as he could manage, and drove off into the night . . .

. . . At precisely the same time as something brightly spiced with lights loomed above Ted Thomas's field, hovered for a moment, and sank below the line of the hedge.

Peter cried, 'They're here!'

'And none before time too,' said Gran. The Martian was already on his feet and hurrying to the door. He paused, trying to take off his sweater. 'You keep that,' said Gran. 'Someone might like to copy the pattern, up where you come from.'

The Martian held out his hand. 'Thank you very much for having me. I've enjoyed it enormously. I wish I could suggest . . . ' He hesitated.

'No, dear,' said Gran. 'Return visits are out, I'm afraid. Foreign travel doesn't appeal to me nowadays. A week in Llandudno in August does me nicely.'

From the field, there was still that whirring noise, and a shimmering orange glow. 'Better go,' said Peter anxiously, 'before anyone comes.'

The Martian nodded. He padded out and down the lane. They saw him get smaller and more indistinct and turn in at the gate into the field and then the orange glow got larger and the whirring louder and there was a snap of bright lights and a rush and then silence and darkness.

Gran closed the door. 'That, I take it,' she said, 'was one of them flying saucers. Pity we couldn't have taken a picture. It would have been nice for my album. Put the torch back in the attic, would you, dear. And put that spanner back in your grandad's toolbox, while you're at it. Good thing we had that by us, or we'd never have been able to lend a hand in the first place. I

21

should have made him up some sandwiches for the journey, you know.'

And she settled down by the stove with her knitting.

This story is by Penelope Lively.

The Seal and the Man of Shetland

Long ago, on the little island of Papa Stour, which lies to the west of the mainland of Shetland in the stormy Atlantic Ocean – long ago there lived a hard-working crofter who owned an old cow and a few scraggy, long-legged sheep which fed on the tough heather and the seaweed on the shore. He had one little field which he planted each year with corn, and three round patches of ground protected from the gales by high walls, in which he grew cabbages, potatoes and turnips.

When the weather was right – which wasn't very often – he would put to sea with his friends to catch what fish they could, and these his wife would clean and roll in oatmeal, and cook over the peat fire.

He was never very rich, and he was often very poor, but generally there was just enough to feed and clothe himself, his wife and his family, and what more, he said, could anyone expect?

But the time came when the winter had been longer and harder than ever before, and his wife looked up from the bannocks she was baking and sighed.

'What worries you, wife?' the man asked.

'The children,' his wife answered. 'They can go barefoot in the summer, but in the winter they need shoes – shoes made from sealskin. They need coats and hoods to keep them warm when the gales blow so strongly that even you can not keep upright – coats and hoods made from sealskin.'

'Have we no money to buy skins from the other fishermen, as we have done before?' the man asked.

'No money at all,' his wife answered.

The man shook his head sadly.

'I have never hunted the seals before,' he said. 'They do us no harm, and there are men who say that the seals are an enchanted people.'

'It is them or us,' his wife said.

'It is them or us,' the man agreed. 'Tomorrow I shall go out with the seal hunters. The children shall have their shoes and coats and hoods.'

Early the next morning, although the sky

was grey and threatening, he went down to the sheltered bay of Hamna Voe where the seal hunters gathered.

'Where are you going today?' he asked.

'To the Ve Skerries,' the captain answered. 'Three miles of hard rowing there, and three miles back. The currents are so dangerous, the tide so treacherous, that the seals think they are safe. If we can only land safely, we shall get all the skins we need for many a long day.'

'My children need shoes and coats and hoods,' the man said. 'Can you do with another pair of hands at the oars?'

'We can,' the captain answered, and the man took his place in the boat with the other fishermen and they set off for the dangerous crags, with the sky growing darker and the gale increasing all the time.

'Hundreds of seals!' one of the fishermen cried as the boat balanced a moment on the crest of a wave, before plunging down into the grey-green trough, and on the next crest the man saw a hollow scooped out of the middle of a great crag, and in the hollow the grey seals basked and slept and grunted in a strangely contented fashion – a sound which the wind carried to the fishermen, above the noise of the

breakers crashing on the rocks and the howl of the gale in their ears.

'Kill and skin as many seals as you can,' the captain cried. 'Work quickly for we can't stay long on the Skerries. I mislike the look of the sky. It is stormy now, but it will be ten times worse before sundown.'

Cautiously they rowed towards the jagged rocks, and then, at the only place where it was possible to land, the captain jumped ashore, the others followed and all pulled the boat up to safety.

26

Quickly the fishermen set to work, and though some of the seals plunged into the sea and escaped, the others had no chance, and before long the boat was loaded with fine sealskins which would fetch a good price on the mainland, and the fishermen knew that they and their wives and children would have plenty to eat and to wear that year.

Darker and darker grew the sky, although it was not time for the setting of the sun, and higher and higher leaped the waves, beating themselves against the Skerries as though they would tear them to pieces.

'We must go now,' the captain shouted.

'The boat isn't fully loaded,' one of the fisher-men protested.

'The load is enough,' the captain answered. 'It's a long pull to Hamna Voe and the sea grows more treacherous each minute.'

The crew hurried to obey their captain, all except this one man, who was some distance away.

'Hurry!' the captain cried. The men launched the boat and tried to keep it to the edge of the crags as the sea tossed it up and down like some new plaything it longed to destroy.

'I am hurrying,' the man answered, slipping

and sliding on the green seaweed as he made his way to the boat. 'I shall be glad to leave the Skerries,' he thought. 'A man must live and provide for his family, but I would rather fish the deep sea than kill the seals.'

Now the great waves battered at the rocks, tearing the boat from its mooring at the very moment that the man was ready to board her, and though time and time again his companions tried to bring her back and take him off, so dan-

gerous were the currents that the captain knew the boat would be dashed to pieces against the jagged rocks and they would all be drowned.

'We will come back for you when the storm is over,' he shouted, and the men pulled and strained on their oars, away from the Ve Skerries and making for their home on Papa Stour.

'Alas!' the man cried, as he watched the boat with his companions and the sealskins disappear into the storm. 'This is the end of me.'

Well he knew that in the Shetlands such a storm as had now arisen might last for days and even weeks, so that by the time his companions could return for him it would be too late, for he had nothing with him to eat or drink, and no other clothes to keep him warm and dry.

'Alas!' he cried. 'Never again shall I see the sweet, green grass of Papa Stour, and the yellow corn, and the purple heather on the steep sides of Hamna Voe. Never shall I see the black lambs skipping on the shore, or watch my wife making bannocks on the peat fire, or see my children laughing as they play among the rock pools.'

Darker grew the sky and fiercer blew the wind as cold, wet and hungry the man sat there lamenting, until presently it seemed to him that, above the roar of the wind and the ceaseless pounding of the sea, there was a new sound – a strange kind of singing, sad but very beautiful.

Closely he listened, peering into the darkness, and as the lightning lit up the sky and the rocks, suddenly he realized that it was the seals who

30

were singing so sadly and so beautifully, the seals which he and his companions had stunned and robbed of their skins. He saw too, that they were no longer seals, but were men and women, tall and fair and strong, and their song was a lament because they had lost their skins. Never again, they sang, could they swim with their friends in the sea; never again could they dive down, deep, deep, to their home, to the city of pearl and coral on the bed of the ocean. Now they were doomed to live like ordinary men and women on earth.

The seals, who had escaped the raid by swimming out to sea as the boat landed, swam slowly back, joining in the sad song, lamenting that never again would they see those whom they loved so dearly, those who, because they had lost their skins, were to be banished from the kingdom of the sea people, to live like ordinary men and women on earth.

'Oh, my dear son,' an old, grey seal cried, swimming up to the Skerries. 'You were all I had in the world, and now you must leave me for ever.'

'Alas, my dear mother,' a handsome young man on the rocks replied. 'Alas for this day and the coming of the seal hunters from Papa Stour, for now I must live on the land for the rest of my days, and never again see you, my mother, or the city of pearl and coral which was our home.'

This is all my fault, the man thought. My companions and I have caused all this unhappiness because we stole their skins.

So guilty and unhappy did he feel that he stood up and was just going to throw himself into the sea, when the old, grey seal looked at him pityingly.

'Poor Man of Shetland,' she said. 'Your companions have left you here without food or shelter, and even now you are thinking that never again will you see your homeland or those you love.'

'Yes,' the man answered sadly. 'That is what I am thinking even now.'

'And the seals on the Skerries with you, they too are thinking that never again will they see their home beneath the ocean, and those they love.'

'Yes,' the handsome young man who was her son answered sadly. 'That is what we are thinking even now.'

'It is my fault that your son and your relations stand here on the Skerries without their seal skins, and so must live on the land for ever,' the man confessed.

'It is your fault in part, and in part it is not your fault,' the old grey seal said. 'Would you undo what you have done?'

'Gladly,' the man answered. 'But it is not within my power. I am a prisoner here on the Ve Skerries. It will be many days before the storm that now rages is spent: too many days, for I shall not be alive when my companions return to rescue me.'

'Man of Shetland,' the old grey seal cried. 'Find the seal skin of my son, so that he can return home again with me, and to repay you, I will save your life.'

'Willingly would I give back the seal skin of your son,' the man answered, 'but it was put in the boat in which my companions rowed away, and even now it will be stored in the little stone house above Hamna Voe, on Papa Stour, and good swimmer though I am, I could not win my way there in this storm.'

'No man can swim as the grey seal swims,' the old seal cried. 'Climb on my back, Man of Shetland, and grip tightly with your hands and your knees, and I will carry you to Papa Stour.'

The man looked down at the smooth, silky coat of the seal, and then at the mountainous waves which plunged and fell on the rocks, and though he was very frightened, he knew he had to do what he was told, to help the young man, and to save his own life.

Into the seething water he plunged, climbing on to the back of the old seal, gripping tightly with his hands and his knees as she swam through the icy waters. Numb were his fingers and exhausted his body when at last he found himself at the far side of Papa Stour, at the foot of a ravine called Akers Geo.

'Hurry and find the skin of my son,' the old seal bade him. 'I shall wait for you here.'

Up the sheer face of the ravine the man climbed, disturbing the kittiwakes and shags which nested there, so that they flew off, flapping their wings in his face, and screaming above the fury of the wind.

Once he gained the top of the cliff, he ran across the wet, green grass, never stopping until he came to the bay of Hamna Voe, and the little stone house in which the seal skins were stored.

Carefully the man looked at the skins, choosing the finest and most beautiful because he knew that this must belong to the handsome young man, and then, with this over his arm, he ran back across the island to the ravine of Akers Geo.

'Here is the skin of your son,' he shouted, throwing it down to the old seal who waited below. 'When I go back, I shall take all the other skins out of the little stone house, and place them on the beach at Hamna Voe. Tell your people to go there for them before daybreak, and then you and your son and all the seal people can return to the city of pearl and coral on the bed of the ocean.'

'Thank you, Man of Shetland,' the old grey seal said. 'The seal people will remember you and yours because of what you have done tonight.'

The next morning, when the hunters saw the man whom they had given up as lost on the Ve Skerries, and heard what had happened and how he had been brought safely back to Papa Stour, they hurried down to the beach at Hamna Voe where the seal skins had been left, but every one had gone, and in their place lay fine salmon, shining mackeral and gleaming herrings, while out at sea the seals played, diving and plunging, swimming and disappearing and reappearing far

35

away in the stormy sea – carefree and happy.

'Never again shall I hunt seals for their skins,' cried the man.

'Neither shall we,' all the other men of the island vowed.

And they and their descendents all kept their promises so that from that time to this the seals sported and played, courted and reared their families in peace on the Ve Skerries, and whenever it pleased them plunged down, unharmed, to their fabulous city of pearl and coral on the ocean bed far below.

This story is by Winifred Finlay.

Tim O'Leary

Hundreds of years ago a goblin sat on the
bank of a river, dipping his toes in the water.
Towards the end of the day, a farmer came
walking home from his fields. When he saw
the little goblin he rubbed his eyes and looked
again.

'What sort of thing are you?' he asked.

'I'm Tim O'Leary,' said the goblin.

'How can that be?' said the farmer. 'Tim
O'Leary's my best friend, and he don't look
a bit like you.'

'Ah!' sighed the goblin. 'I found a cave that
was full of witch's treasure, and I would have
carried it all off, but I cut my feet on some
magic rocks, and turned into a goblin as you
can see.'

'But what are you doing with your feet in
the river?' asked the farmer.

'I'm trying to wash the magic off my feet,' replied the goblin, 'but it's no good.'

'Oh deary me, Tim,' said the farmer, 'whatever can we do?'

'The only way to turn me back into Tim O'Leary is to steal the witch's treasure and throw every single bit of it into the deepest ocean.'

'I'll do that!' cried the farmer.

'But mind you don't cut your feet on the magic rocks!' said the goblin.

'I won't,' said the farmer, 'I have on my toughest boots.' And he set off to find the cave.

It was almost night when he found it, so he lit a torch and ventured in. First he came to a long tunnel, where the floor and the walls and the ceiling were all of sharp rocks. So he walked very slowly and very carefully along the tunnel, and he managed to get to the other end of it without cutting himself.

There he found three great doors. One was made of wood. One was made of iron. And one was made of stone. Just as he was wondering which one to try, he heard a croak behind him. He turned round and found a frog sitting on a rock.

'You want to know what lies behind the doors?' asked the frog.

'Yes,' said the farmer.

'Very well, I'll tell you, if you promise to give me a jewel from the witch's treasure.'

'I can't do that,' replied the farmer, 'I have to throw every single bit of the witch's treasure into the ocean, so that the goblin can turn back into Tim O'Leary.'

'Huh!' said the frog. 'Don't believe that goblin. He's no more Tim O'Leary than I am. He just wants to get his hands on the witch's treasure.'

'Well, why doesn't he come and get it himself?' asked the farmer.

'He's a water-goblin,' said the frog. 'Very powerful, you know, but he must keep touching water. That's why he sits with his toes in the river.'

Well, the farmer didn't know who to believe, but he said to himself: 'I set out to save Tim O'Leary, and that's what I'll do.'

'Come,' said the frog, 'you can give me a jewel from the witch's treasure and then keep the rest for yourself.'

'No,' replied the farmer, 'I must save Tim O'Leary.'

40

'You fool!' screamed the frog, shaking with anger. Then he grew larger and larger, and turned brown and then black and suddenly there was a little old elf.

'You fool!' he screamed. 'You'll never get the witch's treasure now! It lies behind one of the doors, but behind another lies a monster that will tear you to pieces, and behind the third lies a hole that will suck you in. Now you won't know which is which and I shan't tell you!' And he disappeared in a puff of smoke that smelt curiously of nettle beer.

Well, the farmer was very frightened, but he was determined to help Tim O'Leary. So he covered himself from head to foot in mud and got a long pole that stretched the length of the three great doors. Then he opened the first door that was made of wood. Immediately there was a whooshing noise and he saw a terrible black hole, and he felt himself being sucked towards it. And suddenly stones and rocks from the cave were flying past him, and all disappearing into that terrible black hole. But the farmer clung tight to his pole, and because it was wider than the doorway it couldn't go through. So the farmer struggled and strained and eventually he managed to shut the door

41

with a great bang, and the sucking wind died down and the cave grew still again.

'Phew!' said the farmer. 'Now which of the next two doors has the treasure, and which has the monster that will tear me to pieces?'

Finally he decided to try the iron door. He opened it very, very cautiously expecting a terrible monster to leap out at him at any moment. But all was quiet. He looked in and found himself gazing into a high hall, lit by candles, and in the centre of the hall was a great iron chest, with a golden lock.

The farmer looked around the hall and there on the wall hung a great golden key. So he took the key and eagerly opened up the treasure chest. Whereupon there was a terrible roar and out jumped a hideous monster with great claws and bulging eyes. And it stretched out its claws to seize the farmer, but, because he was all covered in mud, he slipped through them, and ran as hard as he could for the door. He got there in the nick of time and slammed it shut just as the monster sprang again, so that it crashed against the great door and the iron rang and the monster roared.

Then the farmer opened the last of the three doors, that was made of stone. And there lay the witch's treasure. The poor man had never seen so many precious stones and so much gold and silver.

'It would be a crime,' he said to himself, 'to throw all that into the ocean but, if that's the only way to save Tim O'Leary, that's what I must do.'

So he put it all into a great sack and carried it down to the river and put it into a boat and set off for the sea.

Well, he hadn't gone very far before he heard singing coming from the back of the boat, and there he found the goblin sitting trailing a toe in the water. In this way, they sailed out into the wide open ocean, until the goblin suddenly said: 'Here we are!'

And the farmer picked up the sack of treasure, and he took one last look at it and said: 'I shall never see such wealth again. But if this is the only way to turn you back into Tim O'Leary, away it goes!' And he emptied all the precious jewels and silver and gold into the sea.

'Ah ha!' cried the goblin. 'Thank you very much! I was never Tim O'Leary and he was never me!' And with that he jumped into the waves and disappeared with the treasure.

Well, the farmer went home, and he found Tim O'Leary sitting on a wall.

'Oh,' said the farmer, 'because of you, I've lost the richest treasure I've ever seen,' and he told him the whole story. And Tim O'Leary put his arm round the farmer and said: 'Leave the treasure to the goblins. You've proved yourself a true friend to me and a true friend I'll be to you, and that's worth more than all the gold and silver and precious jewels in the world.'

This story is by Terry Jones.

The Flood

The shed was near the house. It was dark because it had only one small window, and that was covered with cobwebs. There were some tools in the shed, a spade and a rake and a hoe, and a pile of old sacks. There was something else as well, that not many people knew about. If you stood quite still in the shed, without moving a hand or a foot, you could hear the crackle of straw and perhaps a tiny cry.

The crackle of straw and the cry came from a box standing in a corner. In the box were a mother cat and her three newborn kittens. The cat's name was Minnie and her kittens were named One, Two and Three. When they were big and could wash themselves and drink milk from a saucer, they would go to homes of their own. Then someone would give them proper names. But One, Two, and Three did very well to start with.

Sometimes a dog barked.

'What is that?' asked One, his little legs shaking.

'It is only Prince, the dog,' purred Minnie. 'He is taking care of us. He barks when he sees a stranger coming.'

Sometimes a door banged.

'What is that?' mewed Two, shuddering like a jelly.

'It is only the wind blowing the door shut,' purred Minnie. 'Now the wind won't get into our snug bed.'

Sometimes the coalman tipped the coal out with a sound like thunder.

'What is that?' cried Three, hiding her face in her mother's fur.

'It is only the coalman,' purred Minnie. 'His coal will make the kitchen fire blaze and burn. I will take you into the kitchen for a treat, when you are bigger, if you are very good.'

A lady named Mrs Plum lived in the kitchen. She wore a white apron. Every day she brought Minnie's meals to her, in a blue dish. When

Minnie had finished her food, the dish was as clean as if it had been washed.

One night, when the kittens were fast asleep, curled like furry balls beside their mother, a storm blew up. The door and window of the shed rattled. The rain fell in floods on the roof. There were terrible claps of thunder and bright, zig-zag flashes of lightning. Even Minnie felt frightened. The river ran at the bottom of the garden, on the other side of the garden wall, and she could hear it roaring by. It sounded like a fierce, growling animal.

'What is wrong? What has happened?' mewed One, Two, and Three.

'I do not know, my dears,' said Minnie. 'But we must go to sleep and not be frightened.'

But Minnie herself was very frightened and so were the three kittens. No one could get to sleep while the storm was raging.

The kittens were so young that their eyes were not yet open. But Minnie's eyes shone like green lamps. She could see, under the door of the shed, a trickle of water. The trickle grew into a puddle. The puddle grew into a wave. The wave came nearer and nearer across the floor. Then it reached the box in the corner.

Minnie did not like water. She did not even like getting her paws wet on the wet grass. She was very, very frightened to see the water creeping under the door and spreading across the whole floor.

If it gets any deeper, she thought to herself, I shall take the kittens in my mouth, one at a time, and jump on to the wheelbarrow, and then up on to the shelf where the flowerpots are stacked. I don't think the water could get as high as that.

The water flowed faster and faster under the door until it was inches deep. Just when Minnie was getting ready to take a kitten in her mouth and spring on to the wheelbarrow, and then on to the shelf, a strange thing happened. The wooden box began to move about. It was floating. It was floating like a boat.

There was a thick layer of straw in the bottom of the box and an old woollen jersey. The kittens stayed dry and warm while they floated in their bed. They did not mind at all because they could not see the water as their eyes were shut.

Suddenly there was a clap of thunder and a great blast of wind. The door of the shed blew

open with a bang. The water rushed in and the box swirled round and round. Then it floated out of the shed into the garden.

The river had risen so high that it swept over the garden wall. The box swished over the wall and sailed along the river which was now wide and deep like a sea. Minnie cuddled her babies close to her while the rain fell in torrents. The kittens were soon fast asleep, and though Minnie was sure she would never get a wink herself, she dozed off as well.

When morning came, they were in a watery world. There was water in front of them. Water behind. Water all round. Minnie did not know there could be so much water in one place. Strange things floated by. Branches of trees which had been torn off by the storm. Tables and chairs and pillows and cushions that had been washed out of houses. Sacks and straw and even a dog-kennel. Minnie was pleased to see that the kennel was empty.

Nothing stopped Minnie from bringing up her kittens as well as she could, so she washed them just as carefully as if they had been on dry land. When she had finished One's face, he mewed in an excited voice: 'I can see! I can see! I can see you and Two and Three and the water and everything!'

He frisked about with joy and Minnie was afraid he might fall out of the box.

Before long, Two and Three could see as well and they spent most of the day calling out: 'What's that? What's that? What's that?' or else: 'Why is the water shiny? Why is it brown?' and many other questions, some of which Minnie could not answer.

Though the kittens were well and happy, Minnie was worried. The kittens were fat as butter and could drink her warm milk whenever they wished. But there was nothing for *her* to eat, no milk – no fish – no liver. Nothing at all.

The other thing that worried her was that she could not bring her children up properly in a box floating on the water. How would they learn to lap milk from a saucer? Or walk upstairs? Or climb trees? Or catch mice? Minnie had brought up so many families of kittens that she knew exactly how the job ought to be done.

Now that the rain had stopped, the floods began to go down. The river was no longer wild and roaring. Hedges and bushes could be seen that had been under the water a few hours before. When the box drifted near the bank and was caught on the branches of a willow tree, Minnie knew what she must do.

Quick as a flash, she snatched up the nearest kitten who happened to be Two, and climbed up the tree with him. She dashed back for One and Three and the little family were soon perched on the damp, slippery branch of a willow, instead of cuddled in a floating cradle filled with straw.

'This is a horrid place!' mewed One.

'I shall fall into the water and be drowned!' mewed Two.

'How are we to sleep without a bed?' mewed Three.

Minnie was not comfortable herself as she was trying to look after three young kittens as well as hold on, but she did not approve of grumbling. 'The river is going down,' she said cheerfully. 'Tomorrow or the next day I shall carry you home, one at a time, in my mouth. Till then, you must be good kittens and do what I tell you.'

'Do you know the way home?' asked One.

'We must have floated a long way in our wooden box.'

Minnie was not certain that she *did* know the way, but she replied firmly: 'Of course I know the way. The river brought us here. I shall just follow the river and it will lead us home. Anyhow, all sensible cats know the way home. They never get lost.'

All day and all night Minnie took care of her kittens. She fed them and washed them and sang to them, and when they slept she kept them from falling off the branch. When they were awake and wanted to play, she told them stories. She told them about the red kitchen fire that ate black coal. She told them about mice with long tails who lived in holes and were fun to chase. She told them about dear Mrs Plum and her white apron and her warm, comfortable lap.

When the *next* morning came, the river had gone right down. The ground was wet and muddy, but it was not under water. They could see the path running along the river bank.

'I shall take one of you home now,' said Minnie.

'Take me!' 'No, me!' 'No, ME!' mewed the

three kittens.

'I shall take Three first because she is the smallest,' said Minnie. 'Now One and Two, be brave and sensible and hold on tightly.'

'What will happen if we fall off?' asked One and Two.

'You would lose one of your nine lives,' said Minnie. 'Then you would have only eight left.'

She took little Three in her mouth, climbed down the tree to the ground, and ran off along the river bank. She felt sure she was going the right way and that every step was bringing her nearer home. The wet mud was cold and nasty to her feet, but she did not mind. If only her three kittens were safe in front of the kitchen fire, she would never mind anything again!

Little Three squirmed and squiggled and seemed to get heavier and heavier. When at last Minnie padded slowly through the gate and up the path to the back door, she could hardly drag one foot after the other.

'Miaow! Miaow!' she cried as loudly as she could. 'Miaow!'

In a second the door opened and there stood dear Mrs Plum in her white apron.

'Oh, Minnie! Minnie!' she cried, gathering Minnie and Three up in her arms, and not minding at all about the mud they left on her apron. 'I thought I should never see you again!'

At first Minnie purred loudly and smiled, but she knew the job was not yet finished. She began to kick and struggle till Mrs Plum put her down on the floor. Then she ran to the back door and mewed for it to be opened.

'I know,' said Mrs Plum. 'I understand. You must go back for the others. Wait a moment and I will come too, I'll just make Three safe and comfortable. I kept a bed ready for you all.'

There, on the hearth-rug, was another box with a soft blanket inside. Mrs Plum cuddled Three into the blanket, and Three sat and stared at the fire with round blue eyes. So *this* was the monster who ate black coal!

Mrs Plum put on her coat and hat and took a basket with a lid and opened the door. Minnie ran ahead so quickly that Mrs Plum could only just keep up. They were both tired when they got to the willow tree. Mrs Plum stood at the bottom while Minnie climbed up and found her two kittens cold and shivering, but quite safe.

'We've kept all our nine lives, Mother!' they called out.

'That's my good kittens!' said Minnie, carrying them down to the ground, where Mrs Plum stroked them and petted them and tucked them into the basket, which was lined with flannel. There was just room for Minnie as well. Then Mrs Plum carried the heavy basket home. She had to change hands when one arm ached.

When they were back in the warm kitchen, Mrs Plum gave Minnie a good meal. She had sardines and a dish of cornflakes and three saucers of milk. Then they all five settled down for a cosy afternoon by the fire. Mrs Plum knitted in her rocking chair, and the three kittens watched the red fire eating coal and stared at the brass rim of the fender and the plates on the dresser and all the other wonderful things.

They kept looking at Mrs Plum's ball of wool.

'I don't know why, but I should like to roll that ball of wool all over the floor,' said One.

'So should I!' said Two and Three.

'That would be very naughty of you indeed,'

said Minnie. 'But I wanted to do just the same when I was a kitten.'

'And did you do it?' asked the three kittens.

'Yes, I'm afraid I did!' said Minnie.

She purred and smiled and dozed, as the clock ticked on the wall and the fire crackled and Mrs Plum clicked her knitting needles.

This story is by Ruth Ainsworth.

Persephone

Demeter was the goddess of the corn and of all growing things. Without her care the barley could not ripen, nor the trees put out new leaf in springtime, nor the flowers bloom. And in her task of tending and renewing sweet pastures and bringing green life out of bare rocks, she was aided by her daughter, Persephone, whose other name was Core, the Maiden. Their favourite place on earth was in Sicily.

Now when she was free to please herself, Persephone's greatest joy was to accompany her friends the nymphs; to wander through the fields picking flowers, and to dance or sing or to while away the time with them in play in the green meadows near the hill-town of Enna. One day she sat with a gay company of her friends weaving garlands of hyacinths and wild lavender and dark-eyed anemones, the bees droning in the asphodel all about them, and the cloud shadows drifting across the sunlit mountain slopes. It seemed to them that one of the shadows was darker than the rest. But it was not until it was almost upon them, sweeping nearer over the grass, that they saw it was no cloud shadow at all, but Hades, Lord of the Underworld, driving his dark chariot drawn by four night-black horses.

Before his coming, the little company scattered and ran like a flurry of fallen leaves raised by the wind, all save Persephone, who remained standing alone on the hillside, as though terror had rooted her white feet to the ground.

Hades had asked many goddesses to share his throne deep under the ground, where no sun ever shone and no birds ever sang, where the only flowers were the cold bright jewels and veined gold of the earth, and the only passers-by were the spirits of the dead; and goddess after goddess had refused him. He was weary of asking, and very much alone; and when he saw Persephone standing also alone, with her eyes as blue as the bell-flowers in her fallen garland and her hair as bright as sun-ripe barley, he determined not to be refused again.

Persephone saw the black horses plunging

towards her, the wavering flame in their nostrils and in their eyes, and the dark and terrible beauty of him who drove them. In the last instant she turned to run, but too late. Hades leaned low towards her as the team thundered by, and caught her up into the chariot with him. And holding her in one arm, despite her cries, he lashed the horses to a faster and faster pace.

In a breath of time they reached the banks of the Cyane river, and the water rose in roaring spate, spreading far over its banks to check them. To drive through that broad and rushing torrent would be madness, but if he turned back, the Lord of the Underworld knew that Demeter might well overtake him, and Demeter robbed of her daughter would not be an enemy to take lightly. But there was a third way. Swiftly, scarce checking the horses, he struck the ground with his terrible twin-pointed spear. Instantly a broad crevice opened among the rocks at their feet, and down through it team and chariot plunged into the darkness.

Persephone, straining back for one last glimpse of the blue sky, tore off her girdle and flung it from her into the river, crying to the water nymphs to carry it to her mother. Then the earth closed behind her, and Hades, gently now that the fear of pursuit was over, held her close and kissed her and tried to calm her, while still the horses dashed on through the darkness, never checking until they reached the foot of their lord's throne.

In the upper world, evening came, and Demeter, returning to her home, found no sign of her daughter there. She waited a while, then went to seek her. Night came, and she kindled a torch from the flames of Etna, and went on searching. All night she roamed the mountain slopes, calling distractedly like a ewe whose lamb has strayed, seeking its young. Morning came, and she quenched her torch and wandered on, now hurrying, now lingering, always calling her daughter's name, with no answer but the mountain echoes.

Day followed day, month followed month, while in her search, she forgot her care of the corn and the green things growing. At last her wanderings brought her to Greece, and to Eleusis. And here, worn out with searching, she sat down by the wayside and bent her head into her hands and wept.

There, the daughters of Celeus the king of that country found her. They did not know her for Demeter of the Corn, for she had assumed the appearance of an old beggar-woman, for her wanderings. But they heard her bewailing the loss of her child, and took pity on her, and begged her to come back with them to the palace. And when she came, they brought out their brother, the baby prince Triptolemus, and set him in her arms, thinking that the care of another child might be the best comfort they could give her for the loss of her own.

Triptolemus was a sickly baby, and looking down at him as he lay in her arms, pity stirred in Demeter for the first time since her loss, and she bent her head and kissed him. And a cry of wonder rose from the princesses and the queen their mother and from all the royal household, for at her kiss, colour and health came into the baby's wizened little face, and they could see that he was well and strong.

In joyful gratitude Metaneira the queen told the strange beggar-woman that since she and no one else had been able to bring health to the little prince, she and no one else should be his nurse from that time forward. A little warmth and a little gladness came to Demeter, for already she loved the baby in her arms.

Alone with him that night, watching him sleeping peacefully, she grieved to think that, being mortal, one day he must die. And she thought she would do still more for him. She had given him health, now she would give him immortality. Carefully she anointed his little body. She crooned over him the needful charms; and then carrying him to the hearth, she laid him gently on the glowing logs, that all that was still mortal in him might be burned away.

But that night the queen lay wakeful, and being anxious she got up from beside the sleeping king and went to see that all was well with the child.

She entered the nurse's apartment in the very moment Demeter had laid Triptolemus on the fire. With a wild shriek, she rushed forward and snatched him up, turned him this way and that to see what harm had come to him, then clutching her to her breast, turned like a wild-cat on the stranger who had tried to do this terrible thing – and saw, in place of the beggar-woman, Demeter of the Corn, with her goddess-splendour shining all about her. 'It is a sad thing that you had so little faith in me,' said Demeter. 'I gave your son health; did you think, then, that I would harm him? Because I had begun to love him, I would have given him immortality. Now he will be strong and well, but he will die like other men, when his time comes for dying.'

And she vanished from the queen's sight, and went on her way.

Still searching for lost Persephone, Demeter returned at last to Sicily, and one day, sitting wearily by a river's bank, she saw something shining among the sedges at her feet. She stooped to see what it might be, and drew out Persephone's golden girdle.

Joy leapt in her, for she knew that the water nymphs must have cast it there for her to find, and she had only to follow the river up stream to come at last, surely, to some news of her daughter. So she set out again, and followed the river on and on, up into the hills, until she came to a little waterfall shaded by oleander trees, and there she sank down to rest.

She was half asleep when the voice of the waterfall began to make words in her heart, and she knew the nymph of the waterfall was speaking to her, and roused herself to listen.

There were many waters under the earth, said the nymph, in little rushes and falls of water-words now lost, now clear again, and there were waters that ran sometimes in the sunlight of the upper world and sometimes in the dark below; and she spoke of the rivers of the Underworld that each had its spring at the foot of Hades' throne: Cocytus which ran salt with the tears of the doomed souls in Tartarus, the black and sacred Styx across which Charon the Boatman ferried the souls of the dead, kind Lethe that brought forgetfulness of the past to the blessed, making them ready for the Elysian Meadows. And then just as Demeter was growing weary of this talk of rivers, the nymph of the waterfall told how once, being forced to plunge through a crack in the rocks to avoid the unwanted love-making of a river god, she had herself sojourned for a while among the dark rivers of the earth's heart and how, while she was there, she had seen Persephone, sitting beside Hades on his throne, holding a torch in her right hand and a pomegranate in her left.

Then her voice was lost for good in the rushing and churning of the waterfall.

So Demeter knew at last that her wanderings and seeking had been all in vain. Persephone was where not even her mother could rescue her and bring her back to the light. The search was ended. But she did not return to her old, long-neglected tasks. Instead, she betook herself to a cave she knew of, and there gave herself up utterly to grief.

No rain fell, and the grain withered in the parched ground, no grass sprang among the rocks, and the cattle died. Soon there was famine in the land, and the starving people cried to Demeter to aid them. But Demeter paid no heed; and when their continued clamour disturbed her mourning she vowed no green thing should grow on the earth without her leave, and that she would give no leave to the smallest meadowside weed, so long as her daughter remained pent in the dark realm of Hades.

Then the people in despair cried to great Zeus himself; to Zeus the Thunderer, the Lord and Father of the gods, who alone was stronger than Hades. And when she heard the people crying to the lord of all the gods, Demeter left her cave at last, and added her voice to theirs.

At first Zeus paid no attention, for he was willing that his brother should have Persephone as queen, but at last he grew weary of the prayers and lamentations that beat like waves about his throne, and he yielded in part. If Persephone had eaten nothing of the food of the dead, if not one morsel had passed her lips during the whole time that she had been in the

Underworld, then she should be free to leave her dark husband's side, and her mother might fetch her back to the sunlight and the world of the living.

Demeter, full of joy, hurried to Avernus, the Gateway of the Underworld, past Cerberus the three-headed dog who guarded it, and who, knowing the decree of Zeus, crouched down to let her by; on and on through the dark until she came to the throne of Hades and saw her daughter behind him with a lighted torch in her right hand, a pomegranate in her left, while the whispering spirits of the dead drifted by.

But when she started forward with out-stretched hands to clasp her daughter as she stepped down from the throne – dark Hades sitting there unmoving with face turned away – one of the spirits cried out that the queen had eaten six pomegranate seeds that very day.

Then a great stillness fell upon the whispering and drifting throng, and all the spirits looked towards the queen. And Demeter with her pleading hands still outstretched and empty, asked, 'My daughter, is this true?' And Hades turned his face and asked, 'My wife, is this true?' And Persephone said, looking straight before her at neither one of them, 'My mother, and my lord, this is true.'

Then Demeter broke into a wild wailing, and the sound of it reached the upper air, and the people heard it and began to wail also, and to lament and cry to Zeus as before.

Now, by all the laws of the gods, Persephone, having tasted food in the Kingdom of the Dead, was lost for ever to the world above. But great Zeus had pity. He gave judgement that for every pomegranate seed, Persephone must abide a month in the Underworld with Hades her husband, but that for the rest of the year she might return to her mother and her friends in the upper air.

Then Persephone laid aside the torch and the pomegranate and set her hand in her mother's, and together they returned to the world of men. But as she went, Persephone looked back towards her dark lord, sitting solitary on his throne.

As they came forth from Avernus the skies were blue and the grass sprang under their feet, flowers unfurled their petals and all the green earth rang with birdsong. And joyfully and tenderly Demeter returned to her old tasks again. The corn ripened and the grazing grew rich and the cattle bore their young.

But when the six months of the year that Persephone might spend on earth were over, and it was time for her to return to Hades in the Underworld and take again her place beside him, the earth turned cold and grey; and Demeter retired again to her cave and sadly waited until it was time for Persephone to come back to her.

And so it was from that time forward. Once in every year Persephone stepped out from the shadows into the world of the living, and men's hearts grew light and they said to each other, 'Look! It is Spring!' Once in every year she left them to return to her lord in the shadows, and they said to each other, 'It grows cold and dark. Winter has come again.'

This retelling of the 'Persephone' legend is by Rosemary Sutcliff.

The Gift Pig

Once there was a king whose queen, having just presented him with a baby princess, unfortunately died. The king was very upset at this, naturally. But he had to go on with the arrangements for the christening just the same, as court etiquette was strict on this point. What with his grief and distraction, however, and the yells of his daughter, an exceedingly lively and loud-voiced infant, the invitations to the christening were sent out in a very haphazard manner, and by mistake two elderly fairies were invited who were well known to loathe one another so much that when they met there was bound to be trouble, though when encountered separately they were pleasant enough.

The day of the christening arrived, and at first all went well. The baby princess was christened Henrietta and behaved properly at the ceremony, crying a little but not too much. Then the whole party of relatives and guests strolled back from the royal chapel to the throne room where the reception was being held; the king noticed with alarm that the two elderly fairies were walking side by side. They seemed to be nodding and smiling in the most friendly way, but when he edged nearer to them he heard one say: 'How very well you are looking, darling Grizel! One wouldn't – by artificial light – take you for a day over two hundred.'

'Hardly surprising since I celebrated my hundred-and-eightieth birthday last week. But how are *you* dear Bella? Do you think it was wise to attend the service in that draughty chapel? You walk with such a limp these days.'

'I am perfectly well, thank you, my love. And one does have one's social duty.'

'Especially when there is a free meal attached to it, tee hee!'

'But I confess I hardly expected to see you here – I understood the king's friends were all intelligent and – well, you know – *creative* people.'

'Creative, my angel? In that case, *do* tell me how *you* qualify for admission?'

Shuddering, the poor king made haste to cut the cake and circulate the sherry in hopes of sweetening these acid ladies. He wished that he could get rid of them before the visitors began to give their christening presents, but saw no way to.

Presently the guests, fairy and otherwise, having eaten every crumb of cake and drunk all the sherry, started depositing their gifts and taking their leave. The baby, pink and good in her cradle, was given whole rooms full of silver and coral rattles, shoals of shawls, bonnets and bootees by the bushel, mounds of matinee jackets and mittens, stacks of embroidered smocks and knitted socks. Besides this, she was endowed with good health, a friendly and cheerful nature, intelligence, and a logical mind.

Then the fairy Bella stepped forward and, smiling at the king, said: 'You must forgive me if my wish is not quite so pleasant as some of the preceding ones, but meeting – ahem – such very odd company in your palace has made me nervous and brought on a migraine. Let the princess rue the day that someone gives her a pig, for if ever that happens she will turn into a pig herself.'

'Moreover,' said the fairy Grizel, coming to

the other side of the cradle, 'she will marry somebody with no heart and only one foot.'

'Excuse *me*, dear, I hadn't finished yet; if you would kindly give me time to speak. The princess will lose her inheritance —'

'I *beg* your pardon; I was going to say that there will be a revolution —'

'*Will* you please be quiet, madam! There will *not* be a revolution – or at least, the princess herself will be lost long before that occurs – she will be poor and unknown and have to work for a living —'

'She'll marry one who has spent all his life in the open —'

'Oh, for gracious' sake! Didn't I just say she would marry somebody with only one foot?'

'The two things are not incompatible.'

'You don't very often find agricultural workers with only one foot.'

'Ladies, ladies!' said the king miserably, but not daring to be too abrupt with them, 'you have done enough harm to my poor child! Will you please continue your discussion somewhere else?'

The feuding fairies took their leave (so exhausted by their exhilarating quarrel that they both went home, retired to bed and died the next day) while, left alone, the poor king hung with tears in his eyes over his beautiful pink baby wondering what, if anything, could be done to avert the various bits of evil fortune that were coming to her. All that seemed to lie in his power was strict censorship of her presents, so as to make sure that she was never given a pig.

This he managed successfully until she was five years old, when her cousin came to stay with her. Lord Edwin Fitzlion was a spoilt self-willed boy of about the same age as the princess; he was the seventh son of a seventh son; his brothers were all much older and had gone off into the world, his father had taken to big-game hunting and hardly ever came home, while his mother, tired of looking after boys and attending to shirts, schools, boots, and bats, was away on a three-year cruise. Lord Edwin had been left in the care of servants.

He was very beautiful, with dark velvety eyes and black hair; much better looking than his fat pink cousin; he was inclined to tease her. One day he overheard two equerries discussing the prophecies about her, and he became consumed with curiosity to see whether she would really turn into a pig if she were given one.

There were considerable difficulties about bringing pigs into the palace, but finally Edwin managed to buy a small one from a heavily bribed farmer; he smuggled it in, wrapped in brown paper and labelled *Inflatable rubber dinghy with outboard pump attachment*. Finding the nursery empty he undid the pig and let it loose, then rushed in search of Henrietta.

'Henry! Come quick, I've brought a present for you.'

'Oh, where?'

'In the nursery! Hurry up!'

With rare politeness he stood aside to let her go in first and heard her squeak of joy as she ran through the door.

'Oh, it's a dear little pig —'

Then there was silence, except for more squeaks, and when Lord Edwin looked through the door he saw two little pigs, absolutely identical, sniffing noses in the most friendly way.

Lord Edwin was sent home in disgrace to his father's castle, where he proceeded to run wild, as his parents were still away. (In fact they never returned.) He spent all his time in the woods, riding his eldest brother's horse, Bayard, and flying his next brother's falcon, Ger. One day when far from home he saw a large hare sitting upright on the other side of a pool. Quickly he unhooded the falcon and prepared to fly her.

The hare said: 'You'll be sorry if you do that.'

'Oh, who cares for you,' said Edwin rudely, and he loosed Ger. But the falcon, instead of towering up and dropping on the hare, flew slantwise across the pond into some thick trees and vanished from view. Edwin's eyes followed the bird in annoyance and perplexity. When he looked back he saw that a little old man with an unfriendly expression was standing on the spot where the hare had been.

'You are a spoilt ill-mannered boy,' the old man said. 'I know all about you, and what you did to your cousin. You can stay where you are, learning a bit of patience and consideration, until a Home Secretary comes to rescue you.'

No one had been particularly fond of Edwin, so nobody missed him or enquired after him.

The king, of course, was heartbroken when he learned what had happened to his daughter. Numerous tests were carried out on the two little pigs, in an attempt to discover which one was the princess. They were put in little beds with peas under the mattresses, but both rummaged out the peas and ate them in the course of the night. Dishes of pearls and potato-peelings were placed in front of them, in the hope that the princess would prefer the pearls, but they both dived unhesitatingly for the potato-peelings. The most eminent pig-breeders of the kingdom were brought in to scrutinize them, but with no result; they were two pink handsome little pigs, and that was all that could be said of them.

'Well,' said the king at length, 'one of them is my daughter, and she must receive the education due to a princess. Someday I suppose she will be restored to her proper shape, as she is to marry a one-footed man, poor dear —'

'The fairy didn't actually say a *man* with one foot,' pointed out the Lord Chamberlain.

'Use your sense, man. What else could it be? Anyway she must have a proper education. It would never do if when she reverted to human shape she knew no more than a child of five.'

So the little pigs sat seriously side by side on two little chairs in the schoolroom and were taught and lectured at by a series of learned professors and eminent schoolmistresses. No one could tell if any of this teaching sank in, for they merely sat and gazed. If asked questions, they grunted.

One day, when the pigs were nearly fifteen,

the king came into the schoolroom.

'Hello, my dears,' he said, 'how are you this morning?' He patted his daughter and her friend, then sat down wearily in an armchair to rest while they had their lunch. Affairs of state were becoming very burdensome to him these days.

A footman brought in two big blue bowls of pigmash, one in each hand. The pigs began to give piercing squeals and rush about frantically, bumping into tables and chairs and each other. Their attendant firmly collared them one at a time, tied a white napkin round the neck of each, and strapped them into two chairs. The bowls were put in front of them and instantly there was such a guzzling and a slupping and a splashing and a slobbering that nobody could hear a word for five minutes until the bowls were empty. Then the little pigs looked up again, beaming with satisfaction, their faces covered in mash.

The footman stepped forward again and solemnly wiped their faces clean with a cloth-of-gold face-flannel. Then they were let out to play, and could be seen through the window whisking about the palace garden with tails tightly curled, and chasing one another across the flowerbeds.

The king sighed.

'It's no use,' he said, 'One must face facts. My daughter Henrietta is *not* an ordinary princess. And her friend Hermione is a very ordinary little pig. I am afraid that no prince, even a one-footed one, would ask for Henrietta's hand in marriage after seeing her eat her lunch. We must send them to a finishing school. They have had plenty of intellectual education – at least I suppose they have – it's time they acquired a little polish.'

So the two pigs were packed off (in hampers) to Miss Dorothea ffoulkes' Select Finishing School for the Daughters of the Aristocracy and Nobility.

At first all went well. The king received monthly reports which informed him that his daughter (and her friend) had learned to walk downstairs with books on their heads, to enter and leave rooms, get in and out of motor cars with grace and dignity, play the piano and the harp, waltz, cha-cha-cha, embroider, and ride sidesaddle.

'Well, I've always heard that Miss ffoulkes was a marvel,' said the king, shaking his head in astonishment, 'but I never thought anyone could teach a pig to ride sidesaddle. I can't wait to see them.'

But he had to wait, for Miss ffoulkes strictly forbade the parents of her pupils to visit them while they were being put through her course of training. The reason for this was that she had to treat the girls with such frightful severity, in order to drill the necessary elegance and deportment into them, that if they had been given the chance they would have implored their parents to take them away. Letters, however, were always written to the dictation of Miss ffoulkes herself, so there was no opportunity of complaining, and at the end of her course the debutantes were so grateful for their beautiful poise that all was forgotten and forgiven.

Miss ffoulkes nearly met her Waterloo in Henrietta and Hermione though. She managed to teach them tennis, bridge, and how to dispose of a canape stick, but she could not teach them flower-arrangement. The pigs had no taste for it; they always ate the flowers.

One day they had been spanked and sent into the garden in disgrace when it was discovered that they had eaten a large bundle of lilies and asparagus-fern which they were supposed to build into a decorative creation. Sore and miserable they wandered down Miss ffoulkes's dreary gravel paths. Simultaneously they were seized by the same impulse. They wriggled through the hedge at the bottom of the garden and were seen no more at the Select School.

Instead of a final report on deportment the king had a note from Miss ffoulkes which said: 'I regret to announce that your daughter and her friend have committed the unpardonable social blunder of running away from my establishment. The police have been informed and will no doubt recover them for you in due course. Since this behaviour shows that our tuition has been thrown away on them, your fees are returned herewith. (Cheque for £20,000 enc.) Your very obdt. srvt. Dorothea ffoulkes.'

In spite of all efforts, the police failed to trace the two little pigs. Advertisements, in newspapers, on television and radio, pictures outside police stations, offers of rewards, brought no replies. The king was in terror, imagining his daughter and her friend innocently strolling into a bacon factory. He gave up all pretence at governing and spent his time in a desperate round of all the farms in the kingdom, gazing mournfully at pig after pig in the hope of recognizing Henrietta and Hermione. But none of the pigs responded to his greetings.

As a matter of fact, Henrietta and her friend had gone no further than the garden of the house next door to Miss ffoulkes. There they had been rootling peacefully (but elegantly because their training had not been wasted) among the roses near the front gate when a young man in a white coat came out of the house, irritably listening to the parting words of a beautiful young lady with flowing dark hair.

'And don't forget,' she was saying earnestly, 'all your last experimental results are in the stack under the five-gramme weight, and the milk for tea is in the test-tube at the left-hand end of the right-hand rack, and the baby amoeba wants feeding again at five. Now I really must fly, for my fiancé becomes very annoyed if he is kept waiting.'

'Goodbye, Miss Snooks,' said the white-coated young man crossly, and he slammed the gate behind her. 'Why in the name of goodness do all my assistants have to get married? Not one of them has stayed longer than three months in the last three years.'

Then his eye fell on the two pigs, who were gazing at him attentively.

'Pigs,' he mused. 'I wonder if pigs could be taught to do the work? Pigs might not be so prone to become engaged. Pigs, would you consider a job as research assistants?'

The pigs liked his face; they followed him into the house, where he instructed them in the research work he was doing on cosmic rays.

'I shall have to teach you to talk, though,' he observed, 'for I can't put up with assistants who grunt all the time.'

He laid aside all his other work and devoted himself to teaching them; at the end of a week he had succeeded, for he was the most brilliant scientist and philosopher in the kingdom. In any case, nobody had ever considered teaching the pigs to talk before.

When they could speak, the professor asked their names.

'One of us is Henrietta and one is Hermione, but we are not sure which is which,' they told him, 'for we were muddled up when we were young.'

'In that case I shall call you Miss X and Miss Y. Miss X, you will look after making the tea, feeding the amoeba, and filing the slides. Miss Y, you will turn away all visitors, keep the cosmic ray tuned, and polish the microscope. Both of you will make notes on my experiments.'

The two pigs now found their education of great value. They could carry piles of books and microscope slides about on their heads, curtsey gracefully to callers as they showed them the door, write notes in a neat little round hand, and play the piano and the harp to soothe the professor if his experiments were not going well. They were all very happy together, and the professor said that he had never before had such useful and talented assistants.

One day, after about five years had passed in this manner, the professor raised his eye from the microscope, rubbed his forehead, looked at Miss Y, industriously taking notes, and Miss X, busily putting away slides, and said: 'Pigs, it occurs to me to wonder if you are really human beings turned into your present handy if humble form?'

'One of us is,' replied Miss Y, tucking her pencil behind her ear, 'but we don't know which.'

'It should be easy to change you back,' the professor remarked. 'I wonder I never thought of it before. We can just switch on the cosmic ray and rearrange your molecules.'

'Which of us?'

'You can both try, and I dare say nothing will happen to one of you.'

'Should we like that?' said the pigs to each other. 'You see we're used to being together,' they told the professor.

'Oh, come, come,' he exclaimed impatiently. 'If one of you is really human, it's her plain duty to change back, and the other one should not stand in her way.'

Thus admonished, both pigs walked in front of the ray, and both immediately turned into young ladies with pink faces, turned-up noses, fair hair, and intelligent blue eyes.

'Humph,' remarked the professor, 'that ray must be more powerful than I had allowed for; we do not seem to have advanced matters much further.'

As the young ladies still did not know which of them was which, they continued to be called Miss X and Miss Y, and as they were very happy in their work they continued to help the professor.

One day Miss Y noticed a number of callers approaching the front door. Though she curtseyed politely and did her best to turn them away, they insisted on entering the laboratory.

'Professor,' said a spokesman, 'we are the

leaders of the Revolution, and we have come to invite you to be the first president of our new republic, since you are undoubtedly the wisest man in the country.'

'Oh, good gracious,' said the professor, very much taken aback and frowning because he hated interruptions to his work, 'whatever possessed you to revolt, and what have you done with the king?'

'We revolted because it is the fashionable thing to do – all the other countries have done it ages ago – and the king retired last week; he has taken to farming. But now please step into the carriage which is waiting outside and we will escort you to the president's residence.'

'If I accept,' said the professor, 'it is understood that I must have unlimited time to pursue my research.'

'Yes yes, you will need to do very little governing; just keep an eye on things and see that justice and reason prevail. Of course you can appoint anybody you choose to whatever government positions you wish.'

'In that case I shall appoint my two assistants, Miss X and Miss Y, to be the Home and Foreign Secretaries. I am certain no one could be more competent.'

The new president's residence turned out to be none other that the castle of the Baron Fitzlion, long since deserted. Here the republican government was set up, and as none of the old officials had been removed from their posts, everything proceeded very smoothly and the professor and his two assistants found ample time to continue their research on cosmic rays.

They were now investigating the use of the professor's ray projector on plant life; one day Miss X took a small portable projector into the woods nearby, proposing to make notes about differences in the ray's effect on coniferous and deciduous trees.

While scribbling in her notebook she heard a sneeze, and looked up to discover that a larch in front of her had developed a head. Two handsome black eyes gazed at her mournfully.

'Are you the Home Secretary?' the head enquired.

'Why yes,' replied Miss X, controlling her natural surprise at such a question being put to her by a tree.

'In that case, would you be so extremely kind as to liberate the rest of me with your camera, or whatever it is?'

'I'm afraid this portable projector isn't strong

enough for that – it only runs off a battery. We shall have to build a larger one beside you and connect it to the mains; that will take two or three weeks.'

He sighed. 'Oh well, I've been here fifteen years, I dare say I can wait another three weeks. No doubt I deserved this fate for turning my poor little cousin into a pig, but I *am* so stiff.'

'Did you turn your cousin into a pig?' said Miss X with interest. 'I suppose that might have been me.'

'Were you turned into a pig?'

'Somebody was; we cannot be sure if it was my friend Miss Y or myself. You see we are not certain which of us is which.'

'Henrietta was to lose her inheritance and go through a revolution.'

'So she has.'

'And be poor and unknown and earn her living.'

'We both do.'

'And marry a man with one foot. I'll tell you what,' said Lord Edwin, who had rapidly developed a tremendous admiration for Miss X's cheerful pink face and yellow hair – such a refreshing contrast to the leaves and branches which were all he had had to look at for the last fifteen years – 'I've only got one foot just now, you're standing at it; so if you marry me it will prove that you are the princess.'

'That's true,' she said thoughtfully, 'and then I shall be able to go and see poor Papa and tell him that I am me; there didn't seem much point in disturbing him until I had some more data.'

So the marriage ceremony between Lord Edwin and Miss X was performed while they were building the full size cosmic ray projector nearby, and as soon as the bridegroom had been released they went to see the king, who was very contented on his farm and had no wish at all to resume governing.

'I have acquired a fondness for pigs after looking at so many,' he said. 'I am sure you young people can manage very well without me.'

So Lord Edwin became Prime Minister (having learned thoughtfulness and civilized behaviour during his long spell in the woods). Miss Y, who was now known to be Hermione, married the professor, and they all governed happily ever after.

This story is by Joan Aiken.

The Manatee

The first time that Totty slept away from home was when he went to stay with his grandfather for one night. He went with his elder sister; they slept in two separate beds in the same bedroom. That night Totty didn't feel at all homesick. After all, he had his sister.

Then Totty went all by himself to spend a night with his grandfather. He had said he wanted to do that.

On that visit, in the afternoon, Totty and his grandfather went to the park together, and Totty's grandfather pushed him high on the swings. Then they came home and had tea with baked beans and ice–cream afterwards.

After tea, Totty's grandfather got out a book of wild animal pictures to show him. Totty's best animals were fierce lions and tigers and jaguars and ravening wolves. Almost at the end

of the book there was a picture of two dark grey creatures lolling in the shallow water of some strange river. They had heavy heads and tiny eyes and huge, bristling upper lips. Their forelegs looked rather like canoe-paddles, and Totty couldn't see any back legs at all.

'They're fish,' said Totty.

'No,' said his grandfather. 'They're not fish. They're animals called Manatees. It says so here.'

Totty stared at the Manatees in the picture, and thought. Then he asked: 'What do Manatees eat?'

But either his grandfather did not want to answer that question, or he did not hear it – he was an old man, and rather deaf. He shut the animal book with a snap and said: 'Time for bed, young Totty!'

So Totty went to bed.

He slept in the same bedroom as before; but, of course, the other bed in it was empty this time. All the same, it had been properly made up with a pillow and sheets and blankets. This was in case Totty's sister had come, too.

Totty's grandfather said good-night to Totty and turned off the bedroom light. He left the bedroom door a little ajar, so that Totty could see the light on the landing outside.

Totty heard his grandfather go downstairs, and then he heard the sound of television. His grandfather would probably watch television all evening.

Totty did not go to sleep. He didn't feel lonely; but, all the same, he thought it would have been nice to have someone sleeping in the other bed. After a while, he got up and went out on to the landing, where it was light. He looked down the stairs. The stairs were painted white, with a narrow brown carpet coming up the middle of them. Totty wasn't used to stairs: his family lived in a flat.

After a while he went back into his bedroom, closing the door again so that it was a little ajar, as before. When he had opened the door to go on to the landing, and now when he almost closed it, the hinges had creaked. Totty's grandfather had already said they needed a spot of oil. He had said this was a little job that Totty and he could do tomorrow morning.

Totty got back into bed, and this time he began to go to sleep. Suddenly he was wide awake again because his grandfather had turned off the television set. Now he could hear his grandfather locking up the house, getting ready to go to bed. His grandfather turned out all the lights. He went to bed.

Now there was no light from the landing, shining through the narrow opening of Totty's door. Everything was dark.

Totty lay awake. He couldn't see anything; but, after a while, he thought he had heard something. He thought he heard a tiny, soft little sound like a *flop* on the stairs – far down, at the bottom of the stairs.

Had he heard it, or hadn't he?

There was no one but himself and his grandfather in the house, so there just couldn't be a person creeping up the stairs.

All the same, he became almost sure that there was someone or something at the bottom of his grandfather's stairs, just beginning to climb them.

He held his breath so that he could listen as carefully as possible, and he shut his eyes, too. As soon as he shut his eyes, he saw quite clearly what it was at the bottom of the stairs, preparing to come up them. It was a Manatee.

The Manatee had lifted its bristly face and was looking with its beady eyes towards the landing upstairs. It had put one of its forelegs on the bottom step of the stairs, and now – a heave of its great, grey weight and it was up the first step.

Totty opened his eyes, and then he couldn't see the Manatee on the stairs any more. He could only see the darkness. He couldn't hear the Manatee, either, but that was because he had to breathe and his heart had to beat; and the sound of his own breathing and the beating of his own heart covered the very slight, soft sound that even the most cunning Manatee would have to make as it came upstairs.

Totty said to himself: 'If I yell and yell, Grandfather will wake up and hear me and come. I'll tell him there's a Manatee on the stairs, and he'll go and look, and say there's nothing there. Then he'll go back to bed, and I shall lie here in the dark again, all by myself, and the Manatee will start coming up the stairs all over again.'

So Totty didn't call to his grandfather – yet.

He didn't make any noise at all that might stop his hearing the Manatee coming up the stairs. He breathed as quietly as he could, and he didn't move any part of his body, to make even the smallest rustle of the sheets.

The Manatee must be reaching the top of the stairs by now.

Totty tried to lie still and silent as a stone.

Now the Manatee would be snuffling round the landing. It found Totty's bedroom door ajar. It didn't find his door by accident: the Manatee was looking for it. It had known that Totty's door would be ajar.

Now, Totty thought, if the Manatee pushes the door wider open to come in, the hinges will creak. If the hinges creak, the Manatee is coming in.

But the Manatee did not push the door wider open. Instead, it began to make itself thin. Totty knew why the Manatee was making itself thin. It made itself thinner and thinner, until at last it was thin enough to slide through the crack of the door into Totty's bedroom.

Now, thought Totty, the Manatee is going to rear up at the foot of the bed. The Manatee is a man-eater. It wants to eat *me*. So yell – yell – YELL —

Totty tried to open his mouth to yell for his grandfather, but his mouth wouldn't open. His teeth, clamped together, kept it shut. In vain he struggled and struggled to open his mouth and yell. As he tried, he thought desperately, suppose I could *persuade* the Manatee not to eat me? Suppose I could persuade it that there was

101

something else that it would be nicer to do?

Totty was thinking hard, and he thought one thing, and the Manatee waiting at the foot of his bed listened to Totty's thought. It paid attention. The Manatee began to heave itself slowly, slowly across the bedroom floor from Totty's bed to the other bed, that was empty. Slowly, slowly – with Totty thinking hard all the time – the Manatee heaved itself up on to the bed. Very carefully indeed, so as not to disturb the bedclothes by a rumple or even a wrinkle, it slipped into the bed between the sheets.

Inside his head Totty heard the Manatee say 'Ah!' in a deep, bristly voice. Then it said: 'How beautifully comfortable!' Then it fell fast asleep.

Totty waited a little while until he was sure the Manatee was asleep. Then he went to sleep, too.

He felt quite safe.

When Totty woke in the morning, the Manatee had gone. In going, it had not marked the cleanness of the sheets on the other bed nor disturbed its smoothness.

Totty went down to breakfast with his grandfather. He asked him a question about Manatees. His grandfather fetched the book of animal pictures, and found the right page. He read what the book said about Manatees.

'"They are slow in their movements,"' read Grandfather.

'Yes,' said Totty.

'"And perfectly harmless."'

'Not man-eating?' said Totty.

'No. It says here that they are vegetarian. They eat only water weeds. They live in water.'

'They never come right out on to dry land and into houses?'

'Never.'

Totty was disappointed. He would have liked to have spent another night in his grandfather's house, with the Manatee sleeping in the bed next to his. It would have been a friendly, comfortable thing to do.

But you couldn't expect a water animal to heave itself up a staircase and into a bed, night after night, even to please a friend. Totty knew that. Once would have to be enough.

This story is by Philippa Pearce.

Clever What's-

A long time ago, before you or I were thought of, a great lord lived in a fine house on a large estate. It was known far and wide that he was the richest man in the county – and the meanest.

A clever rascal, travelling the country roads, heard the story and decided he would hire himself out as a servant to this rich man so he went to the gates of the house and asked to speak to the master.

'What is your name?' said the gatekeeper.

'Tell his lordship I'm just a poor traveller.'

'I let no one in unless I know his name,' replied the big gatekeeper, swinging his keys.

'Well, it's like this,' said the crafty fellow, 'it's such a silly name, I'm ashamed to tell anyone. It's "Me–Myself".'

The gatekeeper smiled secretly but he took

his master.

at do you want?' asked his lordship. 'Tell
e and be quick about it.'

'I'm a good worker, my lord, and I should
like to serve in your household.'

'What is your name?'

'I'd rather not say, my lord.'

'Come, come,' said his lordship, impatiently,
'I cannot have a nameless servant. Tell me
your name.'

'Well, sir, it's such a foolish name, I hardly
like to tell folk. It's "Hold–Me–Back".'

The rich man waved his new servant away
and they took him down to the kitchens to
start work immediately. The head cook spoke
to him.

'And who might you be?' he asked. 'What's
your name?'

'If you must know,' sighed the new servant,
'it's "The Cat".'

He and the other servants had a busy time of
it, rushing to and fro while the great lord and his
family ate all they could manage. When they had
finished, the newcomer was given his supper –
cold porridge, and not much of it. He was very
hungry and determined to find something better

to eat as soon as everyone had gone to bed, but the kitchen maid was suspicious and would not leave him. At last, he pretended to fall asleep by the fire. The maid was still suspicious and ran to her master and knocked on his door.

'My lord,' she called, 'The Cat wants to sleep by the fire.'

'Then let him, you silly girl,' replied his lordship.

The kitchen maid went to bed and the crafty servant helped himself to everything he fancied.

The next morning, he got up very early for he knew he must leave the house before anyone found out what he had done. He helped himself to a good few other things, just for good measure, but as he slipped out of the kitchen, the cook discovered him. In a moment, the house was in an uproar. His lordship saw the rascal running across the courtyard, and ran after him, shouting, 'Hold-Me-Back! Stop Hold-Me-Back!'

The servants obeyed their master at once and held him back. What a rage he was in! He shook them off at last and ran towards the gate.

The gatekeeper did his best but he could not

stop the crafty servant who gave him one great push and sent him toppling into the overflowing ditch.

'Who did it?' bellowed the master, arriving just too late.

'Me–Myself, Me–Myself,' groaned the gatekeeper.

'You fool!' shouted his lordship. 'Instead of catching that thief, you throw yourself in a ditch!'

But by that time, the clever rascal had disappeared and was never seen in that part of the country again.

This is a traditional French tale retold by Pat Thomson.

The Three Sisters

There was once a rich king. So rich was he that he believed his riches could never come to an end, and he simply wasted them in foolishness – he played on a golden board with silver skittles. Then one fine day it fell out that all his great wealth was gone. So he had to pawn one town and castle after another, till at last he had nothing left but one old castle away in the woods. He betook himself there with the queen and the three princesses, and led a miserable life with scarce a thing to eat but potatoes, which appeared on the table day after day.

Now the king thought he would go hunting and perhaps bag a hare; so, stuffing his pouch with potatoes, he set forth. But nearby was a great forest no man ever dared enter, as dreadful tales were told of what had happened to those who had done so: bears had devoured them, eagles pecked out their eyes, wolves, lions and other savage beasts lain in wait for them. But the king was not afraid and went straight into the forest.

To begin with he saw nothing unusual; only the mighty shapes of the trees, with all silent below. After tramping awhile, he felt hungry, and sat down comfortably under a tree, ready to eat his potatoes. Just then a bear shuffled out of a thicket, shambled towards him and grunted,

'How dare you sit under my honey-tree! You shall pay dearly for that.'

This gave the king such a fright that he handed his potatoes to the bear to calm him down a little. But the bear just growled, 'Don't like your potatoes! I'd rather eat *you*! Nothing can save you . . . unless, perhaps, you give me your eldest daughter. And – if you do, I'll give you a hundredweight of gold as well!'

The king, in dread of being eaten, answered, 'Yes, you can have her – only do let me go!' At this the bear showed him the way, growling after him, 'In seven days from now I'll fetch my bride.'

But the king went home with an easy mind, thinking to himself the bear couldn't possibly squeeze through a keyhole, and certainly nothing else would be left open.

Once back at the castle, the king ordered all gates to be shut and drawbridges to be raised. He bade his daughter be of good courage, and, to keep her quite safe from the bear-bridegroom, he gave her a small closet high up in the turret to hide in till the seven days were over.

However, on the seventh morning very early, when everyone was still asleep, a splendid carriage arrived at the castle, drawn by six horses and attended by many horsemen clad in gold livery. When it drew up, the drawbridges lowered of their own accord and the locks sprang open without a key. Then the carriage drove on into the courtyard and a handsome young prince stepped down. When the king, awakened by the clatter, looked out of his window, he saw the prince fetch his eldest daughter out of the locked room and lift her into the carriage.

He could only call after her:

'Adieu! Adieu! Dear daughter fair!
Adieu! Adieu! Bride of the Bear!'

From the carriage his daughter waved to him with her little white handkerchief, then away they sped as if harnessed to the wind – straight into the magic wood!

But the king was heartbroken at having given his daughter to a bear; and, with the queen, he wept for three whole days, so sad was he. But on the fourth day, when he had wept enough, he felt that what was done could not be undone, and went down to the courtyard. There he found an ebony chest, terribly heavy to lift. Soon, recalling what the bear had promised, he opened it – and there lay a hundredweight of gold, glittering and sparkling. At the sight of the gold the king felt comforted, and soon redeemed his towns and his realm. Then he wasted his riches on trifles as unwisely as before. This lasted as long as the hundredweight of gold, when again he had to pawn everything, go back to the castle in the wood, and eat potatoes.

Now the king still had a falcon, which he took one day into the fields to hunt for something better to eat. But the falcon rose and flew towards the dark magic wood, which the king no longer dared enter.

The falcon had hardly got there when an eagle shot out of the wood and pursued it. It flew back to the king, who tried to ward off the eagle with his spear, but the bird snatched the spear from him and broke it like a reed. The eagle next crushed the falcon with one of his talons, while with the other he clawed the king's shoulder, crying, 'Why do you invade my kingdom of the air? For that you must die, unless you give me your second daughter as wife.' To this the king answered, 'Yes, you can have her; but what reward do I get?'

'Two hundredweight of gold,' said the eagle;

'and in seven weeks I shall come and fetch her.'

Then the eagle let go of him and flew back to the wood.

The king was grieved to have sold his second daughter also to a wild beast, and dared not tell her what he had done. Six weeks passed by, and in the seventh the princess went down to a lawn in front of the castle to sprinkle her linen with water – when suddenly a splendid train of handsome knights came riding up. The handsomest knight, who rode at the head, dismounted and cried,

'Mount quickly, mount quickly,
O maiden so fair;
Come with us, come with us,
Eagle–bride of the Air.'

Before she could reply, he had lifted her on to his horse and was galloping off with her to the wood, like a bird.

'Adieu! Adieu!'

Long did they wait in the castle for the princess, but never, never did she return.

116

At length the king confessed that one day, when in dire need, he had promised his daughter to an eagle; and the bird must have claimed her. Then, after his sorrow had passed off a little, the eagle's promise came back to his mind. Down he went to the courtyard, and on the lawn he found two golden eggs, each of a hundredweight. A suitor who had so much gold was good enough for him, he thought, and quickly drove all grief from his mind.

The merry life began again, and lasted until the two hundredweight of gold was spent. The king then returned to the castle in the woods, and the only princess left had to boil the potatoes.

The king had no wish to hunt any more hares in the wood, or birds in the air; but he would dearly have liked some fish! So he bade the princess make him a net. He went to a pond not far from the wood, and, finding a boat, he got into it and cast his net. In one haul he caught a great pile of fine red-spotted trout. But when he tried to drag the boat to land it stuck fast and simply would not move, do what he might.

Suddenly a huge whale came puffing along, and snorted, 'How dare you catch my subjects! It will cost you your life!' With that he opened wide his great jaws as if to swallow both king and boat. When the king beheld those dreadful jaws his heart sank. Then he remembered his third daughter, and cried, 'Spare my life, and you shall have my youngest daughter.'

'Very well,' snorted the whale, 'and I'll give you something in return, too. I haven't any gold – don't think much of it! – but the bottom of my lake is paved with pearls; and you shall have three bags full. In the seventh month I shall come and fetch my bride.' And he vanished beneath the water.

Then the king drifted ashore and took his trout home with him. But when they were fried, he couldn't bring himself to eat a single one! For when he looked on his daughter, the only one left and the fairest and dearest of them all, he felt as if a thousand knives were stabbing at his heart.

Six months passed like this, and the queen and princess could not make out what was wrong with him: not once had he looked the least bit happy. In the seventh, the princess was standing one day in the courtyard, filling a glass of water at the fountain, when a carriage drew up with six white horses, and in it were silver-clad figures. A prince got down from the carriage, so handsome that she had not seen a finer man in all her life. He asked for a glass of water. When she gave him the one she was holding in her hand, he threw his arms round her and lifted her into the carriage. Then out of the gate they went and across the fields to the pond.

'Adieu! Adieu! O maiden rare;
Adieu! Adieu! Whale-bride so fair!'

The queen stood at her window and just caught sight of the carriage in the distance. When she could not find her daughter, her heart grew heavy, and she called and searched for her everywhere – but nowhere was she to be heard or seen. Then she knew the truth and began to weep. The king now confessed that in all likelihood a whale had taken their daughter away; for he had been forced to promise her to the beast, and that was why he had been so unhappy all along. Hoping to comfort the queen, he told her about the great riches they would be receiving in return. But the queen would not listen to a word, saying that her only remaining child meant more to her than all the riches in the world.

Now while the Whale Prince was carrying off the princess, his servants put three heavy sacks into the castle. The king found them standing by the door, and when he opened them, he saw they were crammed with beautiful large pearls the size of the biggest peas. So in a trice he was as rich as ever, or even richer, and he redeemed his towns and castles. This time, however, he did not go back to his old life of wasteful folly, but remained sober and thrifty. For when he thought of how his three dear daughters might be faring with their wild beasts – who had perhaps already devoured them – he had no spirit left. Nor could the queen be comforted: she wept more tears for her daughter than the pearls given for her by the whale.

Then bit by bit the sorrow eased, and indeed after a while the queen quite brightened up when she gave birth to a fine boy. As the Lord had sent the child so unexpectedly, they called him Reinald, the Wonder Child. He grew tall and strong; and often the queen would tell him about his three sisters and how they were held in thrall in the magic wood by the three animals.

When he was sixteen, the boy asked the king for a suit of armour and a sword. With these he was ready to set forth on his adventures. So he blessed his father and mother, and went off.

He took his way straight to the magic wood, with only one thought – to find his sisters. But for a long time he wandered about the forest without meeting man or beast; till, after three days, he caught sight of a young woman sitting before a cave. She was playing with a bear-cub, and another very young one was lying in her lap. Thinking, 'Surely that must be my eldest sister,' Reinald tethered his horse and walked up to her. 'Dearest Sister, I'm your brother Reinald, and I've come to visit you.'

The princess gazed at him, and as he looked the image of her father, she did not doubt his words; but, almost frightened out of her wits, she cried, 'O dearest Brother, if you care anything for your life, flee from here as fast as you can. Should my husband, the bear, come home and find you here, he will devour you without pity.'

But Reinald answered, 'I'm not afraid, and will not leave you before I hear all about you.'

When the princess saw she could not persuade him, she led him into the cave, which was dark and a real bear's den. On one side he saw a heap of leaves and straw where the old bear and his cubs slept, while on the other was a fine bed of red and gold cloth for the princess. She bade Reinald hide under the bed, and handed him down some food.

A little later the bear came home. 'I smell, I smell the flesh of a man,' he growled and made as if to poke his big head under the bed. At that the princess replied, 'Oh, do be quiet! whoever could get in here?'

'I came upon a horse in the wood and have made a meal of it,' grumbled the bear, the blood still dribbling from his jaws. 'With the horse goes a man – and I can smell him.' Again he made a move towards the bed, but the princess landed him such a kick that he turned a somersault, then sidled to his bedding, thrust a paw into his mouth, and fell fast asleep.

Each seventh day the bear took on his natural shape and became a handsome Prince, while his cave changed into a fine castle and the beasts of the wood into his servants. It was on one such day that he had fetched the princess. Charming girls had received her at the castle, there had been a lavish feast, and she had fallen off to sleep full of happiness. But when she had woken again, it had been to find herself in a gloomy bear's den with her husband turned back into a bear growling at her feet.

Only the bed and the things she had touched remained unchanged. So for six days she lived in misery, but on the seventh she was comforted; and as she was not growing old – for only the one day counted towards her age – she was not discontented with her life. She had borne her husband two princes, who also were bears for six days, but took on human form on the seventh. Each such seventh day she used to stuff her bedstraw with the most tempting food, cakes and fruit, on which to live through the coming week. The bear was biddable, and did whatever she asked him.

Now when Reinald awoke, he was lying in a silken bed, and servants came to attend him and clothe him in the richest robes, for the seventh day had just come round again. His sister, with the two comely princes and his brother-in-law the bear, came in and were glad to see him. All was fair and noble, and the whole day passed in sweetness and joy.

But in the evening the princess said, 'Dear Brother, make haste now to escape. At day-break my husband will turn into a bear again, and, if he finds you here in the morning, he won't be able to help his nature, but will eat you.'

Just then the Bear Prince came up and gave him three hairs taken from a bear, with the words, 'When you are in need, rub these, and I'll come to your aid.'

They kissed each other goodbye, and Reinald climbed into a carriage drawn by six black horses and drove off. Up hill and down dale he went, up and down, through forests and desert places, hedges and thickets, without pause or rest till morning came; then the skies began to lighten – and Reinald found himself of a sudden lying on the ground. Carriage and horses had melted away, and in the dawn he saw six ants galloping off, drawing a nutshell.

As he was still in the magic wood, he thought he would go in search of his second sister. For three days he wandered about in the wilderness without success, but on the fourth he heard the beating of a great eagle's wings as it swept by to settle on its nest. So he hid in the bushes and waited for it to fly off again; and, sure enough, after seven hours it rose. He came out of hiding, stood under the tree and called, 'Dearest Sister, if you are up there, let me hear your voice. I am Reinald, your brother, and have come to visit you.'

Soon a voice called down, 'If you are Reinald,

my dearest brother, whom I have never seen, pray come up here to me.'

Reinald tried to climb up, but found the trunk too broad and slippery. Thrice he made the attempt and failed; when a silken ladder came down on which he mounted to the eagle's nest, which was firm and strong like a platform built on a lime-tree. His sister was sitting under a canopy of rose-coloured silk, and in her lap lay an eagle's egg which she was keeping warm for hatching. They kissed in greeting and were overjoyed; but after a little while the princess said, 'Now, dearest Brother, make haste and leave again. If the eagle, my husband, finds you, he will peck your eyes out and devour your heart – he has already done that to three of your servants who were out in the wood looking for you!'

'No,' answered Reinald, 'I am staying till your husband changes his shape.'

'That won't be for another six weeks; but, if you can put up with it, I'll hide you in the trunk of the tree, which is hollow, and will get food to you each day.'

Reinald squeezed inside the trunk, the princess let food down to him daily, and, when the eagle flew off, he climbed out to her.

Then after six weeks the change took place, and Reinald awoke in a bed – the same as at his bear brother-in-law's, except that now all was even more splendid. So for seven days he lived very happily with the Eagle Prince, but on the seventh night they bade each other farewell. The eagle gave him three eagle feathers and said, 'When you are in need, rub these, and I'll come to your aid'; then he told his servants to go with Reinald and show him the way.

Now when morning came the servants suddenly vanished, and Reinald found himself alone on a high and dreadful cliff. He looked about him and saw in the distance the shining surface of a great lake gleaming in the first rays of the sun. He thought of his third sister and how she would be down there, and at once started the descent, working his way bit by bit among bushes and rocks. This took him three whole days, and he often lost sight of the lake, but on the morning of the fourth he reached the shore, and called, 'Dearest Sister, if you are down there, pray let me hear your voice. I am Reinald, your brother, and have come to visit you.' But no one answered: all was still.

Next he scattered breadcrumbs on the water and said to the fishes, 'Dear fishes, please go down to my sister and tell her that Reinald the Wonder Child is here and wishes to see her.' But the red-spotted trout snatched at the crumbs without heeding his words.

Then he saw a boat, cast off his armour and, with no more than his glittering sword in his hand, jumped on board and rowed away. He had drifted for some time when he saw sticking out of the water a chimney made of rock-crystal, from which came a pleasant smell. He rowed towards it, thinking that surely it must be there his sister lived, climbed into the chimney, and went shooting down. The princess started up in alarm at suddenly seeing a pair of legs swaying in the fireplace, but then the whole man appeared and made himself known as her brother.

She was delighted, but soon her face clouded over and she said, 'The whale heard you were going to visit me, but feared that, if you came while he was a whale, he wouldn't be able to help swallowing you. He'd smash my crystal house, and I'd perish in the floods myself.'

'Can't you hide me till the spell is broken?'

'Impossible! How could I? Can't you see that all the walls are crystal-clear?'

However, she thought and she thought, till at

last she remembered the room where they kept the firewood. She stacked the wood so close that nothing could be seen from the outside, then hid the Wonder Child safely. Soon after the whale came home, and the princess trembled like an aspen leaf. He swam time after time round the crystal house, and, when he caught sight of part of Reinald's jacket peeping out from under the wood, he thrashed with his tail, gave a terrifying snort, and would have smashed the house had he seen more.

Every day he came and swam once round, but at length, in the seventh month, the spell duly broke. Reinald then found himself in a castle surpassing even the eagle's in splendour. It stood in the middle of a fair island. There for a whole month he lived in sheer delight with his sister and brother-in-law. When the month was over the whale gave Reinald three scales and said, 'When you are in need, rub them, and I'll come to your aid.' Then he had Reinald taken to the shore, where he found his armour again.

For seven days the Wonder Child roamed through the wilderness, and for seven nights he slept under the stars. In the end he caught sight of a castle, which proved to have an iron gate with a huge lock to it. A black bull with glowing eyes guarded the entrance, and Reinald rushed on the beast and dealt it a fierce thrust in the neck; but, as this was made of steel, the sword splintered like glass. He next tried with his spear, and it broke like straw. The bull then tossed him in the air with its horns, and he landed in the branches of a tree. Now in dire need, he bethought him of the three hairs of the bear and rubbed them in his hand. On the instant a bear came shambling along, turned on the bull and rent it in pieces – when, lo and behold! a duck rose from the entrails and flew rapidly off.

Reinald next rubbed the three eagle feathers, and at once a mighty eagle swept through the air after the duck as it made straight for a lake, and swooping down upon it, seized and devoured it. But Reinald noticed that, a little before, the duck had dropped a golden egg into the water. So he rubbed the three scales in his hand, and at once a whale came swimming along, swallowed the egg, and spat it on to the land.

Reinald took it up and broke it open with a stone, to find inside a little key, the very key to open the iron gate. Indeed, when he just touched the lock with it, the gate sprang open by itself, and he entered. The bolts on the further doors,

too, shot back of their own accord, and through seven doors he entered seven noble rooms, all brightly lit, till in the last he saw a maiden lying on a bed asleep. So lovely was she that he was quite blinded by her beauty.

Reinald tried to waken her, but failed, for she slept as soundly as if she were dead. In a temper he hit a black board next to the bed, and that very moment the maiden awoke, only to fall asleep again the next. At this he picked up the board and flung it down on the stone floor so that it smashed into a thousand pieces.

Hardly had that happened when the maiden opened her eyes wide – the spell was broken. It chanced that she was the sister of Reinald's three brothers-in-law, and, as she had refused her love to a wicked wizard, he had put her into a death-like sleep and changed her brothers into beasts. The spell was to last as long as the black board remained unbroken.

Reinald now led the maiden into the open air, and when they were outside the gate his brothers-in-law came riding up from three sides, the spell on them broken, and on their wives and children too. The Eagle-bride, having hatched her egg out, carried a lovely baby girl in her arms.

All then went to the old king and queen; and so the Wonder Child had brought his three sisters home. Shortly after, he married the beautiful maiden, and there was joy and happiness everywhere – and now:

The cat runs Home –
My Tale is done.

This story is by The Brothers Grimm, translated by Ruth Michaelis-Jena.

The Cheeseburger

I always look forward to the times when my grandma comes to stay. She's my dad's mum and she comes from a little fishing village in Northumberland, and she's small and round and cuddly. You should hear the lovely funny way she talks. Sometimes you can't understand what she's talking about, and my dad has to translate. And when she's here for a holiday she never stops cooking from the minute she arrives until the minute she leaves because she's convinced that my dad and I don't get enough to eat.

'Ee, hinny,' she says, poking me in the ribs. 'There's not a scrap of meat on them bones of yours. We'll soon fettle that.' And she rolls her sleeves up and puts a pinny on and sets to work baking scones and stotty cakes and the yummiest minced beef and potato pies you ever tasted. And my dad has the time of his life, until Grandma goes home again and he has to go straight back on his diet.

One Saturday morning during the Easter holidays my mum was out shopping and my dad was at the barber's getting his hair cut, what there is left of it, that is. And my grandma and I were having a great old time rolling out pastry and baking apple turnovers and jam tarts and stuff. I was glad to be indoors in our nice cosy kitchen on such a nasty cold day, especially with my grandma for company. She was cutting out the circles of dough and I was putting them in the tray and spooning dollops of jam into them. Quite a lot of the jam was finding its way into my mouth.

'Give over, our Charlie,' said my grandma, rapping my knuckles with a wooden spoon. 'You'll not want any dinner. And then it'll be me gets the blame from your mam.'

Just then there was a loud bang at the back door and Angela stuck her head in.

'Hi, Charlie,' she said. 'Hi, Mrs Ellis. Coo, it's lovely and warm in here.'

Angela came in and shut the door. 'It's freezing out there. What shall we do, Charlie?'

I scowled at her, not feeling pleased to see her at all. I was quite happy as I was. But she had come round specially to see me and I supposed I could hardly just tell her to go away. My grandma could though. She's never been all that fond of Angela.

'You can both get away upstairs out of my way,' she said, shooing Angela and me out of the kitchen.

'Let's play in your room,' said Angela. So we went upstairs.

Angela had brought her new radio cassette player with her, and as soon as we were in my room she switched it on.

'We don't need the radio on,' I said. 'Come on, we'll have a game of draughts.' And I started to pull the board and the box of draughts from under my bed. I like playing draughts with Angela because I usually win. It's the only game she hasn't worked out a way of cheating at.

'We can listen while we play,' she said. 'This is ever such a good programme, Charlie. It's a new local radio station.'

So we set up the draughts while the radio churned out pop music. I was just starting to get interested in the game when Angela suddenly leaned over and turned up the volume.

'What was that?' she said. 'Listen. They're talking about our village.'

The voice sounded strangely familiar, in spite of the vague American accent that all disc jockeys and telly announcers seem to have these days, but what really made my ears prick up was the word cheeseburger. Cheeseburgers are one of the things I love best in the whole world.

'. . . to celebrate the thirtieth anniversary of our international hamburger company,' the voice was saying. 'Don't miss this opportunity. Sample our new giant MacDougal Cheeseburger. Entirely free of charge. In the following MacDougal branches today. Thames Street, Cookburn. The Parade, Edgebourne. And West Street, Barlow. Taste a free MacDougal Cheeseburger TODAY!'

There was a sort of click and a crackle and then more music. I stared at Angela and Angela stared at me. The draught board lay forgotten between us.

'Charlie,' she said slowly. 'Did you hear what I heard? Free giant cheeseburgers? The Parade, Edgebourne. Wowee!'

I could almost taste those onions already. 'Come on, Angela,' I said. 'We can be there in two minutes.'

We tumbled helter-skelter down the stairs and out of the back door, shouting ''Bye, back in a minute,' to my astonished grandma as we went.

We reached our gate and Angela, instead of coming with me, turned towards her own house.

'I'd better just pop home and tell my mum where I'm going,' she said. 'You run ahead and get a place in the queue. There's bound to be thousands of people.'

So I tore off along the street as fast as I could go, and I was in such a hurry that I didn't look where I was going and collided with Miss Menzies coming out of her gate. Miss Menzies is the fattest person I know, and it knocked the wind clean out of me, I can tell you. It was a bit like colliding with an elephant.

'Charlie,' gasped Miss Menzies, going as red as her knitted wooly hat. 'What's all the hurry?'

'Sorry,' I said hastily, trying to get my breath back. 'I'm in a bit of a hurry. They're giving away free cheeseburgers at MacDougal's in the Parade.'

'They're what?' squealed Miss Menzies, her little piggy eyes lighting up greedily. 'Are you sure?'

'It's just been on the radio,' I said. And I set

off again with Miss Menzies lumbering along behind me, all her rolls of fat wobbling with the effort. It's amazing how fast fat people can run when there's free food at the end of it.

I reached the High Street and ran past the paper shop, and who should be coming out but that fat fool Laurence Parker and that nice David Watkins who's going to be an astronaut when he grows up. Remember that story about Henny Penny running around telling everybody the news when the sky fell on her head? Well, that's just how I felt, puffing out the story of the free cheeseburgers all over again, while the two of them stood there with their mouths open.

'Garn. You're having us on,' jeered Laurence Parker. 'Free cheeseburgers. What a load of cogglewoggle.' He took David's arm. 'Come on, Dave. She's pulling a fast one. You know what she's like, her and that Angela Mitchell.'

'It's true,' I insisted, feeling hurt. 'Honest. Cross my heart. It was on the radio, only five minutes ago.'

The two boys stared at me for a moment.

'It won't do any harm to go and look,' said David at last.

'All right,' said Laurence. 'But I'm warning

you, Charlie Ellis. If this is a hoax, you're not half in for it.'

Miss Menzies had just about caught up by now, and the four of us hurried round the corner into the Parade, expecting to find an enormous crowd outside MacDougal's.

There was nobody there. We all stood outside, peering stupidly in through the window and gasping and panting for breath. Two elderly ladies drinking tea stared back in surprise. And two youths in motorcycle jackets and boots stopped eating their sausage, egg and beans and made rude signs at us through the glass.

'It was on the radio,' I said helplessly. 'Angela heard it too. It was her radio,' I added, as if that made the slightest bit of difference.

'Well, there's no point in standing out here,' said Laurence Parker sensibly. 'Let's go in and ask.'

So we all trooped in and went up to the counter where a chef with a black droopy moustache and a white apron and a tall white hat was sharpening a long steel knife. He opened his mouth wide and hooted with laughter when I asked in a small voice about free cheeseburgers and I could see all the fillings in his teeth.

'Nar. There's nothing like that happening

around here. MacDougal's never give nothing away, far as I know.' He called over to the waitress, busily wiping tables in the corner. 'You know anything about it, Betty?' The waitress shook her head.

'Somebody having you on, I expect,' said the chef. 'But I can rustle you up a few cheese-burgers, if that's what you're after. One pound twenty pence each.'

Nobody had any money and we all shuffled out, red in the face. Miss Menzies looked as if she was about to cry. And I don't know what Laurence Parker would have done to me if my dad hadn't come out of the barber's shop just at that moment.

'Dad!' I shouted, and flung myself at him. I've never been so pleased to see him in my life.

'Charlie,' he said, looking cross. 'What are you doing? Out in the cold with no coat on? I thought you were at home helping Grandma.'

And so I had to tell the whole story all over again, with the others standing around butting in now and again with rude remarks.

'And now nobody believes me,' I said helplessly. 'But it *was* on the radio. Cross my heart.'

My dad scratched his head and looked baffled. 'You must have made a mistake, pet. Perhaps you got the day wrong or something.'

'That's all very well,' grumbled Miss Menzies. 'But she's made me run all this way for nothing.'

Laurence Parker and David Watkins marched away up the street making disgusted faces. My dad smiled at Miss Menzies soothingly.

'Come on,' he said. 'I'll buy you a Cheeseburger. The biggest one they've got.' And Miss

Menzies brightened up at once.

Well, of course by then I was so upset I couldn't have eaten a cheeseburger to save my life. So we left Miss Menzies happily tucking in and set off home, expecting to meet Angela on the way back.

'I can't understand it,' I said. 'She only went to tell her mum where we were going. She should have caught up by now.'

My dad made a grim face and shook his head. 'It all sounds a bit fishy to me,' he said. 'I still reckon it's one of her tricks. And I wouldn't mind having a look at that radio of hers,' he added, as we went in the back door.

So while my dad was telling my grandma all about it, I ran upstairs to my room. I picked up the radio and carried it down to the kitchen.

'It's still switched on,' I said to my dad. 'But it's making ever such a funny noise. A sort of whispery, scratchy noise.' My dad took it from me and pressed some of the switches.

'Just as I thought,' he said. 'Listen to this Charlie. It's not the radio at all. It's a tape.'

He pushed the rewind button and the tape whizzed back to the beginning. And my mouth fell open as the same pop music I'd heard earlier filled the kitchen. Then a sudden click, a crackle, and a voice.

'Hurry, all you Edgebourne cheeseburger fans. Try a free giant MacDougal cheeseburger today. To celebrate the thirtieth anniversary of our international hamburger company. Don't miss this opportunity . . . '

My dad switched off the tape and the three of us sat down at the kitchen table looking glum. There was a long silence.

'It was Angela's Uncle Peter's voice,' I said weakly. 'I recognize it now. She must have got him to help her. I bet they're both laughing their socks off by now.'

'Well, what a nasty trick to play on a friend,' said my grandma, pursing her lips. 'That Angela wants her behind tanned, if you ask me.' Then a sudden gleam came into her blue eyes and she jumped to her feet.

'We'll fettle them,' she grinned, fastening her pinny more firmly round her waist and pushing a stray wisp of white hair out of her eyes. 'Cheeseburger, was it? I'll show 'em cheeseburger.' And my dad and I watched in astonishment as she banged the frying pan on the stove and went into action.

She put four beefburgers and some chopped onion in the frying pan and while they were sizzling away she cut open a whole stotty cake. And if you've never seen a stotty cake it's a sort of flat round bread roll about the size of a dinner plate. My grandma spread the stotty cake with butter, then put the slices of cheese on it and popped it under the grill to brown. When the cheese was all bubbly she crammed the four beefburgers together on one half of the stotty cake and plonked the other half triumphantly on top.

'There,' she said, her face all pink. 'Show that to your fine friends next door.'

I looked at it and giggled. It was the biggest cheeseburger in the world, and I couldn't wait to see Angela's face. I put on my anorak and my woolly hat, hung Angela's radio by its strap on my shoulder, and picked up the enormous cheeseburger.

It was so big it took two hands to hold it. My dad had to open the door for me to let me out, and my grandma was laughing so much she had to keep wiping her eyes on her apron.

Anyway, I strolled round the corner and sauntered into Angela's drive. I stood leaning

against the gate where I knew I could be seen from the windows, and I started taking great bites out of that cheeseburger.

'Yum, yum,' I kept saying loudly, and it wasn't long before a face appeared at the window. Angela's Uncle Peter. And his eyes bulged out of his head when he saw what I was eating.

Then the back door opened and Angela came rushing out.

'Flippin' heck,' she said. 'Where did you get that?'

'Um . . . yum . . . er . . . I brought your radio back,' I said, with my mouth full. I waved the cheeseburger under her nose so she could smell those onions and that lovely toasted cheese. 'Best cheeseburger I ever tasted,' I said, taking another huge bite and licking melted butter off my wrist. 'Pity you didn't get there in time.'

Angela looked so flabbergasted I almost choked. She hung on the gate beside me and watched enviously.

'Go on, Charlie. Give me a bit,' she wheedled. 'You're never going to manage all that by yourself.'

146

I don't know how I did it but I did. I ate it all. Every scrap. Right down to the last bite. And I didn't give her one single crumb. I was so full I almost burst, but it was worth it just to see her face.

This story is by Sheila Lavelle.

Unicorn

Rhiannon was an orphan and lived with her grandmother in a village at the edge of the forest. She was one of Sir Brangwyn's orphans, as they called them in those parts – that is to say her parents were alive but her father was imprisoned in the dungeons of Castle Grim and her mother worked in the castle kitchens to earn money to pay for his food. He had done nothing wrong, but Sir Brangwyn had accused him of stealing deer. Sir Brangwyn liked to have the best men from all the villages in his dungeons, so that the other villagers would stay quiet and good, and hardly dare murmur when he taxed them of every farthing they had. Everyone knew that Rhiannon's father was innocent. If he had really been stealing deer Sir Brangwyn would have hanged him from the nearest tree.

Rhiannon was not allowed to go with her

parents to the castle. Sir Brangwyn made a point of leaving the children behind, to remind the other villagers to be good. So she stayed in the village and did her share of the work. Everybody in the village had to work or starve, and since Rhiannon was only nine her job was to hunt in the forest for truffles.

The forest was enormous – nobody knew how big, or what lay deep inside it. Some said that strange beasts laired there, dragons and unicorns and basilisks, which could turn you to stone by looking at you. Others said all that had happened in the old days, and the strange beasts were gone, so now there were only ordinary animals such as boars and deer and wolves and bears. Sometimes Sir Brangwyn would come and hunt these. Hunting was the one thing he cared about in all the world.

Rhiannon never went deep into the forest. She always stayed where she could see the edge. Truffles are hard to find. They are a leathery black fungus which grows underground on the roots of certain trees, and for those who like rich food (as Sir Brangwyn did) they add a particularly delicious taste and smell. Rhiannon always hoped that one day she would find so many truffles that Sir Brangwyn would send her parents home as a reward, but it did not happen. She seldom found more than a few, and sometimes she would dig in forty places and find none.

Exactly a year after the soldiers had come to take her father away, Rhiannon went off to the forest as usual. But not at all as usual, she was followed back that evening by a small white horse, no more than a foal, pure silvery white with a silky mane and tail.

The villagers were amazed.

'It must have escaped from some lord's stable,' they said, and they tried to catch it, thinking there would be a reward. But before they came anywhere near, away it darted, glimmering across the meadows and into the dark woods. Then they found, to their further amazement, that Rhiannon's basket was full of truffles.

'My little horse showed me where to dig,' she said.

This seemed very good news. Sir Brangwyn's tax-clerk would be coming to the village in a few day's time. Truffles were rare and expensive. Perhaps they could pay all their taxes in truffles, and that would mean they would have a little food to spare for themselves this year.

So next morning a dozen men and women went up with Rhiannon to the forest, hoping the little horse would come and show them where to dig. But they saw no sign of it and they found nothing for themselves, so at noon they went back to their own tasks, leaving Rhiannon behind. Again that evening the white horse came glimmering behind her almost to the edge of the village, then dashed away. And again Rhiannon's basket was full of truffles.

So it went on every day until the tax-clerk came, and the headman brought him a whole sackload of truffles to pay the taxes. This clerk was a monk, who could read and write. He knew things which ordinary people did not know. When he asked how it happened that the village had so many truffles to send, the headman told him. The headman was a simple fellow. (Sir Brangwyn saw to it that the clever ones were in his dungeons.)

That evening the clerk sent for a hunstman and told him what he wanted, and next night the huntsman came back and told what he had seen. He had followed Rhiannon up to the forest, taking care to keep out of sight, and at the forest edge a little white horse had come cavorting out and kissed Rhiannon on the forehead, and then she had followed it in under the trees where it had run to and fro, sniffling and snuffling like a dog, and every now and then it would stop and paw with its hoof on the ground, and Rhiannon would dig there and find truffles. The horse was obviously extremely shy of anyone but Rhiannon and kept looking nervously around, so the huntsman had not been able to come close, but then, when Rhiannon's basket was full, she had sat down with her back against a tree and the horse had knelt by her side and put its head in her lap and gazed into her eyes and she had sung to it. The little horse had been so entranced that it seemed to forget all danger, and the huntsman had been able to creep close enough to see it well.

'And sure, it's a very fine wee beast, your honour,' he said to the clerk. 'What it'll be doing in these woods I can't be guessing. And it's never seen bit or bridle, I'll be bound, never seen stall nor stable. As for the colour of its coat, it is whiter than snow, not a touch nor fleck of grey nor of yellow in it. Only one thing . . .'

'Yes?' whispered the clerk, as though he knew what was coming.

'The pity of it is the animal's face, for it's

misshapen. It has this lump, or growth as it might be, big as my bent thumb between the eyes.'

'Ah,' said the clerk.

Next morning he left his tax-gathering and hurried to Castle Grim to tell Sir Brangwyn there was a unicorn in the woods.

The great hall of Castle Grim was hung with the trophies of Sir Brangwyn's hunting. Deer and hare, boar and badger, wolf and fox, heron and dove, he had ridden it down or dug it up or hawked it out of the air. But he had never hunted unicorn. Before the clerk had finished his message Sir Brangwyn was on his feet and bellowing for his huntsmen and his grooms, and in an hour he was on the road with a dozen expert trackers and twenty couple of hounds.

The people of Rhiannon's village were glad to see him come. Sometimes when a village had shown him good sport he had let the people off their taxes for a whole year. So here they were eager to help. They beat the woods, they dug traps where they were told, they set watch, but it was all no use. Sir Brangwyn's clever hounds bayed to and fro and found nothing. His trackers found the prints of an unshod foal all over the truffle-grounds, but lost the trail

154

among the trees.

After three days of this Sir Brangwyn's temper soured, and the villagers began to be anxious. Then the tax-clerk explained what Sir Brangwyn had been too impatient to hear before, that the only way to hunt a unicorn is to send a maiden alone into the woods, and the unicorn will come to her and lay its head in her lap and be so enraptured by her singing that he will not see the huntsmen coming.

Sir Brangwyn had not brought any maidens with him, but the village headman told him about Rhiannon. All that night the villagers toiled by torch-light, cutting brushwood and building a great bank of it by the truffle-grounds, high enough to hide a mounted man. In the morning they took Rhiannon up to the forest. When they told her what she had to do she tried to say no, but by this time Sir Brangwyn had learnt where her parents were, and he explained to her what would happen to them if she refused. So she went into the forest and sat down, weeping, in her usual place, while Sir Brangwyn waited hidden behind the bank of brushwood.

For a long while everything was still.

Then, suddenly, there was a glimmering deep

in the dark wood and the unicorn came delicately out, looking this way and that, hesitating, sniffing the wind. When it was sure all was safe it cavorted up to Rhiannon and kissed her on the forehead and knelt by her side with its head on her lap, gazing up into her eyes, puzzled why she did not sing. Sir Brangwyn broke from his hide, spurring the sides of his horse till the blood runnelled. The nearing hooves drubbed like thunder.

Then Rhiannon could bear it no more. She jumped to her feet with her arms round the unicorn's neck, dragging it up, and turned its head so that it could see Sir Brangwyn coming.

At once it reared away, giving Rhiannon no time to loose her hold. The movement twitched her sideways and up so that she was lying along the unicorn's back with her arms round its neck and the unicorn was darting away under the trees with Sir Brangwyn hallooing behind, his spear poised for the kill.

The hoofbeats dwindled into the forest, into silence. Then huntsmen and villagers, waiting out of sight beyond the forest, heard a voice like the snarl of trumpets, a man's shout and a crash. Then silence once more.

The trackers followed the hoofprints deep

156

into the dark wood. They found Sir Brangwyn's body under an oak tree, pierced through from side to side. His horse they caught wandering close by.

Rhiannon came out of the forest at sunset. What had she seen and heard? What fiery eye, what silvery mane? What challenge and what charge? She would not say.

Only when her mother and father came home, set free by Sir Brangwyn's heir, she told them something. They had taken her to her bed and were standing looking down at her, full of their happiness in being all three together again, and home, when she whispered four words.

'Unicorns have parents too.'

This story is by Peter Dickinson.

Handsel and Gristle

Once a plum a time, in the middle of a forest, there lived a poor woodnutter and his woof. They lived in a little wooden sausage with their two children, Handsel and Gristle. The one was called Handsel because he had huge hands and the other was called Gristle because it was all gristly.

One day the woodnutter came home and he says: 'I've been nutting wood all day long but I couldn't sell Lenny.'

(No one knew who Lenny was, no one asked him and no one has ever found out.)

Anyway, that night the children went to bed with puffin to eat.

Downstairs, the woodnutter and woof talked. The woodnutter says, 'How can we feed the children? They've gone to bed with puffin to eat again.'

'Quite,' says woof, 'that's what I was stinking. There's only one thing we *can* do – take them off to the forest and leave them there.'

'But that would be terrible,' said the woodnutter. 'They might die of gold, they'd sneeze to death out there. Or they might starve and die of Star Station.'

'Well,' said woof, 'they might die of Star Station here. We've got no money because you went nutting wood all day and couldn't sell Lenny.'

(There's Lenny again.)

What the woodnutter and woof didn't know, was that Handsel and Gristle were still a cake and they could hear everything the woodnutter and woof were sighing.

Later that night, when everybun was in bed, asweep, Handsel crept downstairs, out into the garden and filled his rockets full of phones and then crept back to bed.

The next day, woof said, 'Right, children, today we're all going to the forest to nut wood.'

They all left the little wooden sausage and off they went.

As they walked along woof noticed that Handsel kept stopping.

'Keep up, Handsel,' woof said. What woof didn't notice was that Handsel was taking the phones out of his rocket and dropping them on the ground.

They walked and walked and walked until in the end they hopped.

'Well,' said woof, 'you two stay here, we've got to go off and nut some wood.' And off they went.

Handsel and Gristle played together for a bit till they felt so tired they lay down and fell asweep.

When they poke up it was bark and they were all abone.

Gristle didn't know where it was, but Handsel said, 'Don't worry, leave it to me,' and there, shining in the spoon-light were the phones all the way back comb.

When they got back, their father was very pleased to see them but woof was very cross.

'Oh, you wicked children, why did you sweep so wrong in the forest. We thought you'd never get back comb.'

That night the woodnutter and woof sat and talked again.

'Well,' said woof, 'we'll just have to try again. We'll take them a long way, bleep into the forest.'

Upstairs Handsel and Gristle were still a cake and they could fear everything their father and woof were sighing.

So later, when everybun was in bed, Handsel staired down crept. But this time the sausage door was locked. He couldn't get out. Sadly he went back to bed.

Curly in the morning, woof got the two children up. 'Right, we're all going off to the forest again to nut wood. Here's some bread for you to eat when we get there.'

And off they went.

As they walked along, Handsel broke off little boots of bread and dropped them on the ground behind them.

'Handsel,' said his father, 'why do you keep shopping?'

'I'm not shopping,' said Handsel. 'We haven't got any money – you couldn't sell Lenny, remember?'

'Who's Lenny?' said the woodnutter.

'Keep up, Handsel,' said woof.

They went bleeper and bleeper into the forest to a place they had never seen before or five.

'We're just going off to nut some wood. We'll come and get you before it gets bark,'

162

said woof. And off they went.

Handsel and Gristle played for a pile and then, when they smelt tired, they went to sweep. When they poke up it was bark.

'Don't worry, Gristle,' said Handsel, 'all we have to do is follow the boots of bread.'

'What boots? What bread?' said Gristle.

'I croak up my bread into little boots,' said Handsel, 'and all we have to do is follow the creadbums.'

But when they started to look for the cread-bums, there weren't Lenny.

(Hello, Lenny.)

You see all the birds of the forest had eaten them. So they walked and walked, lay down, walked and walked and walked – but they were lost. They walked some more and suddenly they came upon a little house.

The whales of the house were made of ginger-bread, the wind-nose were made of sugar and the tyres on the roof were made of chocolate.

Handsel and Gristle were so hungry that they ran up to the house and started to break off bits of the chocolate tyres and sugar wind-nose.

Then all of a sudden, a little old ladle came out of the house.

'Oh, what dear little children, come in, come

in. You look so hungry. I'll give you something to beat.'

She took them inside and gave them a huge pile of cancakes.

Handsel and Gristle thought they were very lucky – what they didn't know was that the little old ladle was really a wicked itch – a wicked itch that lay in wait for children. The itch then killed them to eat.

When Handsel and Gristle finished their cancakes, the itch took hold of Handsel's hand (which was very easy considering how big it was) and before he knew what had happened, the itch threw him into a rage in the corner of the room.

'Aha, I'm a wicked itch,' said the little old ladle, 'and you'll stay in that rage till you're nice and cat. And as for you,' said the itch to Gristle, 'you can fleep the swore.'

'Who swore?' said Gristle. 'Not me.'

'Shuttup,' said the itch, 'or I'll eat your eyes.'

Now, this itch couldn't see very well. In fact, most itches can't see very well and Gristle noticed this.

Every day, the itch watched Handsel's rage and the itch said, 'Hold out your finger, boy.

I want to know if you're getting cat.'

'Are we getting a cat?' said Gristle.

'Shuttup,' said the itch, 'or I'll eat your nose.'

It was about this time that Gristle told Handsel that the itch couldn't see. (Which Handsel knew all along because all the itches he knew just itched and nothing much else.)

Anyway, because of this, Handsel didn't hold out his finger for the itch, he yelled out a bone instead.

'Not ready yet,' the itch said.

Well, four weeks passed by and the itch said, 'I can't wait this pong. You're cat enough for me.'

'He's nothing like a cat,' said Gristle.

'Shuttup,' said the itch, 'or I'll eat your lips.'

Then the itch told Gristle to fill a kettle of water and light the fire in the gloven. When Gristle got back, the itch said, 'Is the fire ready?'

'I don't know,' said Gristle.

'Stupiddle thing,' said the itch. 'I have to do everyping round here.'

Then the wicked itch went right up to the gloven door, but Gristle was just behind and Gristle gave the itch one pig push; the itch went flying into the gloven; Gristle slammed the door, and that was the end of the wicked itch.

Then Gristle ran over to Handsel and got him out of his rage.

'Handsel, we're free,' said Gristle.

'Three?' said Handsel. 'There's only two of us now you've got rid of the itch.'

But they were so happy they hugged and missed and danced and sank all round the room.

Then they filled their rockets full of bits of chocolate tyres, gingerbread whales and sugar wind-nose and ran back through the forest to the woodnutter's little sausage.

When he saw Handsel and Gristle, he was overjointed. Woof was dead by now, so Handsel and Gristle and the old woodnutter lived afferly ever harpy.

(And they never did sell Lenny.)

This story is by Michael Rosen.

Rikki-Tikki-Tavi

At the hole where he went in
Red-Eye called to Wrinkle-Skin.
Hear what little Red-Eye saith:
'Nag, come up and dance with death!'

Eye to eye and head to head,
   (Keep the measure, Nag.)
This shall end when one is dead;
   (At thy pleasure, Nag.)
Turn for turn and twist for twist —
   (Run and hide thee, Nag.)
Hah! The hooded Death has missed!
   (Woe betide thee, Nag!)

This is the story of the great war that Rikki-tikki-tavi fought single-handed, through the bathrooms of the big bungalow in Segowlee cantonment. Darzee, the tailor-bird, helped him, and Chuchundra, the musk-rat, who never comes out into the middle of the floor, but always did the real fighting.

He was a mongoose, rather like a little cat in his fur and his tail, but quite like a weasel in his head and his habits. His eyes and the end of his restless nose were pink; he could scratch himself anywhere he pleased, with any leg, front or back, that he chose to use; he could fluff up his tail till it looked like a bottle-brush, and his war-cry, as he scuttled through the long grass, was: '*Rikk-tikk-tikki-tikki-tchk!*'

One day, a high summer flood washed him out of the burrow where he lived with his father and mother, and carried him, kicking and clucking, down a road-side ditch. He found a little wisp of grass floating there, and clung to it till he lost his senses. When he revived, he was lying in the hot sun on the middle of the garden path, very draggled indeed, and a small boy was saying: 'Here's a dead mongoose. Let's have a funeral.'

'No,' said his mother; 'let's take him in and dry him. Perhaps he isn't really dead.'

They took him into the house, and a big man picked him up between his finger and thumb, and said he was not dead but half choked; so they wrapped him in cotton-wool, and warmed him, and he opened his eyes and sneezed.

170

'Now,' said the big man (he was an English-
man who had just moved into the bungalow);
'don't frighten him, and we'll see what he'll
do.'

It is the hardest thing in the world to frighten
a mongoose, because he is eaten up from nose
to tail with curiosity. The motto of all the
mongoose family, is 'Run and find out'; and
Rikki-tikki was a true mongoose. He looked at
the cottonwood, decided that it was not good
to eat, ran all round the table, sat up and put
his fur in order, scratched himself, and jumped
on the small boy's shoulder.

'Don't be frightened, Teddy,' said his father.
'That's his way of making friends.'

'Ouch! He's tickling under my chin,' said
Teddy.

Rikki-tikki looked down between the boy's
collar and neck, snuffed at his ear, and climbed
down to the floor, where he sat rubbing his
nose.

'Good gracious,' said Teddy's mother, 'and
that's a wild creature! I suppose he's so tame
because we've been kind to him.'

'All mongooses are like that,' said her husband. 'If Teddy doesn't pick him up by the
tail, or try to put him in a cage, he'll run in

and out of the house all day long. Let's give him something to eat.'

They gave him a little piece of raw meat. Rikki-tikki liked it immensely, and when it was finished he went out into the veranda and sat in the sunshine and fluffed up his fur to make it dry to the roots. Then he felt better.

'There are more things to find out about in this house,' he said to himself, 'than all my family could find out in all their lives. I shall certainly stay and find out.'

172

He spent all that day roaming over the house. He nearly drowned himself in the bath-tubs, put his nose into the ink on a writing-table, and burnt it on the end of the big man's cigar, for he climbed up in the big man's lap to see how writing was done. At nightfall he ran into Teddy's nursery to watch how kerosene-lamps were lighted, and when Teddy went to bed Rikki-tikki climbed up too; but he was a restless companion, because he had to get up and attend to every noise all through the night, and find out what made it. Teddy's mother and father came in, the last thing, to look at their boy, and Rikki-tikki was awake on the pillow. 'I don't like that,' said Teddy's mother; 'he may bite the child.'

'He'll do no such thing,' said the father. 'Teddy's safer with that little beast than if he had a bloodhound to watch him. If a snake came into the nursery now—'

But Teddy's mother wouldn't think of anything so awful.

Early in the morning Rikki-tikki came to early breakfast in the veranda riding on Teddy's shoulder, and they gave him banana and some boiled egg; and he sat on all their laps one after the other, because every well-brought-up mongoose always hopes to be a house-mongoose some day and have rooms to run about in, and Rikki-tikki's mother (she used to live in the General's house at Segowlee) had carefully told Rikki what to do if ever he came across white men.

Then Rikki-tikki went out into the garden to see what was to be seen. It was a large garden, only half cultivated, with bushes as big as summer-houses of Marshall Niel roses, lime and orange trees, clumps of bamboos, and thickets of high grass. Rikki-tikki licked his lips. 'This is a splendid hunting-ground,' he said, and his tail grew bottle-brushy at the thought of it, and he scuttled up and down the garden, snuffing here and there till he heard very sorrowful voices in a thorn-bush.

It was Darzee, the tailor-bird, and his wife. They had made a beautiful nest by pulling two big leaves together and stitching them up the edges with fibres, and had filled the hollow with cotton and downy fluff. The nest swayed to and fro, as they sat on the rim and cried.

'What is the matter?' asked Rikki-tikki.

'We are very miserable,' said Darzee. 'One of our babies fell out of the nest yesterday, and Nag ate him.'

'H'm!' said Rikki-tikki, 'that is very sad – but I am a stranger here. Who is Nag?'

Darzee and his wife only cowered down in the nest without answering, for from the thick grass at the foot of the bush there came a low hiss – a horrid cold sound that made Rikki-tikki jump back two clear feet. Then inch by inch out of the grass rose up the head and spread hood of Nag, the big black cobra, and he was five feet long from tongue to tail. When he had lifted one-third of himself clear of the ground, he stayed balancing to and fro exactly as a dandelion-tuft balances in the wind, and he looked at Rikki-tikki with the wicked snake's eyes that never change their expression, whatever the snake may be thinking of.

'Who is Nag?' said he. '*I* am Nag. The great god Brahm put his mark upon all our people when the first cobra spread his hood to keep the sun off Brahm as he slept. Look, and be afraid!'

He spread out his hood more than ever, and Rikki-tikki saw the spectacle-mark on the back of it that looks exactly like the eye part of a hook-and-eye fastening. He was afraid for the minute; but it is impossible for a mongoose to stay frightened for any length of time, and though Rikki-tikki had never met a live cobra before, his mother had fed him on dead ones, and he knew that all a grown mongoose's business in life was to fight and eat snakes. Nag knew that too, and at the bottom of his cold heart he was afraid.

'Well,' said Rikki-tikki, and his tail began to fluff up again, 'marks or no marks, do you think it is right for you to eat fledglings out of a nest?'

Nag was thinking to himself, and watching the least little movement in the grass behind Rikki-tikki. He knew that mongooses in the garden meant death sooner or later for him and his family, but he wanted to get Rikki-tikki off his guard. So he dropped his head a little, and put it on one side.

'Let us talk,' he said, 'You eat eggs. Why should not I eat birds?'

'Behind you! Look behind you!' said Darzee.

Rikki-tikki knew better than to waste time in staring. He jumped up in the air as high as he could go, and just under him whizzed by the head of Nagaina, Nag's wicked wife. She had crept up behind him as he was talking, to make an end of him; and he heard her savage hiss as the stroke missed. He came down almost across her back, and if he had been an old mongoose he would have known that then was the time to break her back with one bite; but he was afraid of the terrible lashing return-stroke of the cobra. He bit, indeed, but did not bite long enough, and he jumped clear of the whisking tail, leaving Nagaina torn and angry.

'Wicked, wicked Darzee!' said Nag, lashing up as high as he could reach toward the nest in the thorn-bush; but Darzee had built it out of reach of snakes, and it only swayed to and fro.

Rikki-tikki felt his eyes growing red and hot (when a mongoose's eyes grow red, he is angry), and he sat back on his tail and hind legs like a little kangaroo, and looked all round him, and chattered with rage. But Nag and Nagaina had disappeared into the grass. When a snake misses its stroke, it never says anything or gives any sign of what it means to do next. Rikki-tikki did not care to follow them, for he did not feel sure that he could manage two snakes at once. So he trotted off to the gravel path near the house, and sat down to think. It was a serious matter for him.

If you read the old books of natural history, you will find they say that when the mongoose fights the snake and happens to get bitten, he runs off and eats some herb that cures him. That is not true. The victory is only a matter of quickness of eye and quickness of foot – snake's blow against mongoose's jump – and as no eye can follow the motion of a snake's head when it strikes, that makes things much more wonderful than any magic herb. Rikki-tikki knew he was a young mongoose, and it made him all the more pleased to think that he had managed to escape a blow from behind. It gave him confidence in himself, and when Teddy came running down the path, Rikki-tikki was ready to be petted.

But just as Teddy was stooping, something flinched a little in the dust, and a tiny voice said: 'Be careful. I am death!' It was Karait, the dusty brown snakeling that lies for choice on the dusty earths; and his bite is as dangerous as the cobra's. But he is so small that nobody thinks of him, and so he does the more harm to people.

Rikki-tikki's eyes grew red again, and he danced up to Karait with the peculiar rocking, swaying motion that he had inherited from his family. It looks very funny, but it is so perfectly balanced a gait that you can fly off from it at any angle you please; and in dealing with snakes this is an advantage. If Rikki-tikki had only known, he was doing a much more dangerous thing than fighting Nag, for Karait is so small, and can turn so quickly, that unless Rikki bit him close to the back of the head, he would get the return-stroke in his eye or lip. But Rikki did not know: his eyes were all red, and he rocked back and forth, looking for a good place to hold. Karait struck out. Rikki jumped sideways and tried to run in, but the wicked little dusty grey head lashed within a fraction of his shoulder, and he had to jump over the body, and the head followed his heels close.

Teddy shouted to the house: 'Oh, look here! Our mongoose is killing a snake'; and Rikki-tikki heard a scream from Teddy's mother. His father ran out with a stick, but by the time he came up, Karait had lunged out once too far, and Rikki-tikki had sprung, jumped on the snake's back, dropped his head far between his fore-legs, bitten as high up the back as he could get hold, and rolled away. That bite paralysed Karait, and Rikki-tikki was just going to eat him up from the tail, after the custom of his family at dinner, when he remembered that a full meal makes a slow mongoose, and if he wanted all his strength and quickness ready, he

179

must keep himself thin.

He went away for a dust-bath under the castor-oil bushes, while Teddy's father beat the dead Karait. 'What is the use of that?' thought Rikki-tikki. 'I have settled it all'; and then Teddy's mother picked him up from the dust and hugged him, crying that he had saved Teddy from death, and Teddy's father said that he was a providence, and Teddy looked on with big scared eyes. Rikki-tikki was rather amused at all the fuss, which, of course, he did not understand. Teddy's mother might just as well have petted Teddy for playing in the dust. Rikki was thoroughly enjoying himself.

That night, at dinner, walking to and fro among the wine-glasses on the table, he could have stuffed himself three times over with nice things; but he remembered Nag and Nagaina, and though it was very pleasant to be patted and petted by Teddy's mother, and to sit on Teddy's shoulder, his eyes would get red from time to time, and he would go off into his long war-cry of '*Rikk-tikk-tikki-tikki-tchk!*'

Teddy carried him off to bed, and insisted on Rikki-tikki sleeping under his chin. Rikki-tikki was too well-bred to bite or scratch, but as soon as Teddy was asleep he went off for his nightly walk round the house, and in the dark he ran up against Chuchundra, the musk-rat, creeping round by the wall. Chuchundra is a broken-hearted little beast. He whimpers and cheeps all the night, trying to make up his mind to run into the middle of the room, but he never gets there.

'Don't kill me,' said Chuchundra, almost weeping. 'Rikki-tikki, don't kill me.'

'Do you think a snake-killer kills musk-rats?' said Rikki-tikki scornfully.

'Those who kill snakes get killed by snakes,' said Chuchundra, more sorrowfully than ever. 'And how am I to be sure that Nag won't mistake me for you some dark night?'

'There's not the least danger,' said Rikki-tikki; 'but Nag is in the garden, and I know you don't go there.'

'My cousin Chua, the rat, told me —' said Chuchundra, and then he stopped.

'Told you what?'

'H'sh! Nag is everywhere, Rikki-tikki. You should have talked to Chua in the garden.'

'I didn't — so you must tell me. Quick, Chuchundra, or I'll bite you!'

Chuchundra sat down and cried till the tears rolled off his whiskers. 'I am a very poor man,' he sobbed. 'I never had spirit enough to run out into the middle of the room. H'sh! I mustn't tell you anything. Can't you *hear*, Rikki-tikki?'

Rikki-tikki listened. The house was as still as still, but he thought he could just catch the faintest *scratch-scratch* in the world — a noise as faint as that of a wasp walking on a window-pane — the dry scratch of a snake's scales on brickwork.

'That's Nag or Nagaina,' he said to himself; 'and he is crawling into the bathroom sluice. You're right, Chuchundra; I should have talked to Chua.'

He stole off to Teddy's bathroom, but there was nothing there, and then to Teddy's mother's bathroom. At the bottom of the smooth plaster wall there was a brick out to make a sluice for the bath-water, and as Rikki-tikki stole in by the masonry curb where the bath is put, he heard Nag and Nagaina whispering together outside in the moonlight.

'When the house is emptied of people,' said Nagaina to her husband, '*he* will have to go away, and then the garden will be our own again. Go in quietly, and remember that the big man who killed Karait is the first one to bite. Then come out and tell me, and we will

182

hunt for Rikki-tikki together.'

'But are you sure that there is anything to be gained by killing the people?' said Nag.

'Everything. When there were no people in the bungalow, did we have any mongoose in the garden? So long as the bungalow is empty, we are king and queen of the garden; and remember that as soon as our eggs in the melon-bed hatch (as they may tomorrow), our children will need room and quiet.'

'I had not thought of that,' said Nag. 'I will go, but there is no need that we should hunt for Rikki-tikki afterwards. I will kill the big man and his wife, and the child if I can, and come away quietly. Then the bungalow will be empty, and Rikki-tikki will go.'

Rikki-tikki tingled all over with rage and hatred at this, and then Nag's head came through the sluice, and his five feet of cold body followed it. Angry as he was, Rikki-tikki was very frightened as he saw the size of the big cobra. Nag coiled himself up, raised his head, and looked into the bathroom in the dark, and Rikki could see his eyes glitter.

'Now, if I kill him here, Nagaina will know; and if I fight him on the open floor, the odds are in his favour. What am I to do?' said

Rikki-tikki-tavi.

Nag waved to and fro, and then Rikki-tikki heard him drinking from the biggest water-jar that was used to fill the bath. 'That is good,' said the snake. 'Now, when Karait was killed, the big man had a stick. He may have that stick still, but when he comes in to bathe in the morning he will not have a stick. I shall wait here till he comes. Nagaina – do you hear me? – I shall wait here in the cool till daytime.'

There was no answer from outside, so Rikki-tikki knew Nagaina had gone away. Nag coiled himself down, coil by coil, round the bulge at the bottom of the water-jar, and Rikki-tikki stayed still as death. After an hour he began to move, muscle by muscle, toward the jar. Nag was asleep, and Rikki-tikki looked at his big back, wondering which would be the best place for a good hold. 'If I don't break his back at the first jump,' said Rikki, 'he can still fight; and if he fights — oh, Rikki!' He looked at the thickness of the neck below the hood, but that was too much for him; and a bite near the tail would only make Nag savage.

'It must be the head,' he said at last; 'the head above the hood; and when I am once there, I must not let go.'

Then he jumped. The head was lying a little clear of the water-jar, under the curve of it; and, as his teeth met, Rikki braced his back against the bulge of the red earthenware to hold down the head. This gave him just one second's purchase, and he made the most of it. Then he was battered to and fro as a rat is shaken by a dog – to and fro on the floor, up and down, and round in great circles; but his eyes were red, and he held on as the body cart-whipped over the floor, upsetting the tin dipper and the soap-dish and the flesh-brush, and banged against the tin side of the bath. As he held he closed his jaws tighter and tighter, for he made sure he would be banged to death, and, for the honour of his family, he preferred to be found with his teeth locked. He was dizzy, aching, and felt shaken to pieces when something went off like a thunderclap just behind him; a hot wind knocked him senseless, and red fire singed his fur. The big man had been wakened by the noise, and had fired both barrels of a shot-gun into Nag just behind the hood.

Rikki-tikki held on with his eyes shut, for now he was quite sure he was dead; but the head did not move, and the big man picked him up and said: 'It's the mongoose again,

Alice; the little chap has saved *our* lives now.' Then Teddy's mother came in with a very white face, and saw what was left of Nag, and Rikki-tikki dragged himself to Teddy's bedroom and spent half the rest of the night shaking himself tenderly to find out whether he really was broken into forty pieces, as he fancied.

When morning came he was very stiff, but well pleased with his doings. 'Now I have Nagaina to settle with, and she will be worse than five Nags, and there's no knowing when the eggs she spoke of will hatch. Goodness! I must go and see Darzee,' he said.

Without waiting for breakfast, Rikki-tikki ran to the thorn-bush where Darzee was singing a song of triumph at the top of his voice. The news of Nag's death was all over the garden, for the sweeper had thrown the body on the rubbish-heap.

'Oh, you stupid tuft of feathers!' said Rikki-tikki angrily. 'Is this the time to sing?'

'Nag is dead – is dead – is dead!' sang Darzee. 'The valiant Rikki-tikki caught him by the head and held fast. The big man brought the bang-stick, and Nag fell in two pieces! He will never eat my babies again.'

'All that's true enough; but where's Nagaina?' said Rikki-tikki, looking carefully around him.

'Nagaina came to the bathroom sluice and called for Nag,' Darzee went on; 'and Nag came out on the end of a stick – the sweeper picked him up on the end of a stick and threw him upon the rubbish-heap. Let us sing about the great, the red-eyed Rikki-tikki!' and Darzee filled his throat and sang.

'If I could get up to your nest, I'd roll all your babies out!' said Rikki-tikki. 'You don't know when to do the right thing at the right time. You're safe enough in your nest there, but it's war for me down here. Stop singing a minute, Darzee.'

'For the great, the beautiful Rikki-tikki's sake I will stop,' said Darzee. 'What is it, O Killer of the terrible Nag?'

'Where is Nagaina, for the third time?'

'On the rubbish-heap by the stables, mourning for Nag. Great is Rikki-tikki with the white teeth.'

'Bother my white teeth! Have you ever heard where she keeps her eggs?'

'In the melon-bed, on the end nearest the wall, where the sun strikes nearly all day. She hid them there weeks ago.'

'And you never thought it was worthwhile to tell me? The end nearest the wall, you said?'

'Rikki-tikki, you are not going to eat her eggs?'

'Not eat exactly; no. Darzee, if you have a grain of sense you will fly off to the stables and pretend that your wing is broken, and let Nagaina chase you away to this bush. I must get to the melon-bed, and if I went there now she'd see me.'

Darzee was a feather-brained little fellow who could never hold more than one idea at a time in his head; and just because he knew that Nagaina's children were born in eggs like his own, he didn't think at first that it was fair to kill them. But his wife was a sensible bird, and she knew that cobra's eggs meant young cobras later on; so she flew off from the nest, and left Darzee to keep the babies warm, and continue his song about the death of Nag. Darzee was very like a man in some ways.

She fluttered in front of Nagaina by the rubbish-heap, and cried out: 'Oh, my wing is broken! The boy in the house threw a stone at me and broke it.' Then she fluttered more desperately than ever.

Nagaina lifted up her head and hissed: 'You warned Rikki-tikki when I would have killed him. Indeed and truly, you've chosen a bad place to be lame in.' And she moved toward Darzee's wife, slipping along over the dust.

'The boy broke it with a stone!' shrieked Darzee's wife.

'Well, it may be some consolation to you when you're dead to know that I shall settle accounts with the boy. My husband lies on the rubbish-heap this morning, but before night the boy in the house will lie very still. What is the use of running away? I am sure to catch you. Little fool, look at me!'

Darzee's wife knew better than to do *that*, for a bird who looks at a snake's eyes gets so frightened that she cannot move. Darzee's wife fluttered on, piping sorrowfully, and never leaving the ground, and Nagaina quickened her pace.

Rikki-tikki heard them going up the path from the stables, and he raced for the end of the melon-patch near the wall. There, in the warm litter about the melons, very cunningly hidden, he found twenty-five eggs, about the size of a bantam's eggs, but with whitish skin instead of shell.

'I was not a day too soon,' he said; for he could see the baby cobras curled up inside the skin, and he knew that the minute they were hatched they could each kill a man or a mongoose. He bit off the tops of the eggs as fast as he could, taking care to crush the young cobras, and turned over the litter from time to time to see whether he had missed any. At last there were only three eggs left, and Rikki-tikki began to chuckle to himself, when he heard Darzee's wife screaming:

'Rikki-tikki, I led Nagaina toward the house, and she has gone into the veranda, and – oh, come quickly – she means killing!'

Rikki-tikki smashed two eggs, and tumbled backward down the melon-bed with the third egg in his mouth, and scuttled to the veranda as hard as he could put foot to the ground. Teddy and his mother and father were there at breakfast; but Rikki-tikki saw that they were not eating anything. They sat stone-still, and their faces were white. Nagaina was coiled up on the matting by Teddy's chair, within easy striking-distance of Teddy's bare leg, and she was swaying to and fro singing a song of triumph.

'Son of the big man that killed Nag,' she hissed, 'stay still. I am not ready yet. Wait a little. Keep very still, all you three. If you move I strike, and if you do not move I strike. Oh, foolish people, who killed my Nag!'

Teddy's eyes were fixed on his father, and all his father could do was to whisper: 'Sit still, Teddy. You mustn't move. Teddy, keep still.'

Then Rikki-tikki came up and cried: 'Turn round, Nagaina; turn and fight!'

'All in good time,' said she, without moving her eyes. 'I will settle my account with *you* presently. Look at your friends, Rikki-tikki. They are still and white; they are afraid. They dare not move, and if you come a step nearer I strike.'

'Look at your eggs,' said Rikki-tikki, 'in the melon-bed near the wall. Go and look, Nagaina.'

The big snake turned half round, and saw the egg on the veranda. 'Ah-h! Give it to me,' she said.

Rikki-tikki put his paws one on each side of the egg, and his eyes were blood-red. 'What price for a snake's egg? For a young cobra? For a young king-cobra? For the last – in the very last of the brood? The ants are eating all the others down by the melon-bed.'

Nagaina spun clear round, forgetting everything for the sake of the one egg; and Rikki-tikki saw Teddy's father shoot out a big hand, catch Teddy by the shoulder, and drag him across the little table with the tea-cups, safe and out of reach of Nagaina.

'Tricked! Tricked! Tricked! *Rikk-tck-tck!*' chuckled Rikki-tikki. 'The boy is safe, and it was I – I – I that caught Nag by the hood last night in the bathroom.' Then he began to jump up and down, all four feet together, his head close to the floor. 'He threw me to and fro, but he could not shake me off. He was dead before the big man blew him in two. I did it. *Rikki-tikki-tck-tck!* Come then, Nagaina. Come and fight with me. You shall not be a widow long.'

Nagaina saw that she had lost her chance of killing Teddy, and the egg lay between Rikki-tikki's paws. 'Give me the egg, Rikki-tikki. Give me the last of my eggs, and I will go away and never come back,' she said, lowering her hood.

'Yes, you will go away, and you will never come back; for you will go to the rubbish-heap with Nag. Fight, widow! The big man has gone for his gun! Fight!'

Rikki-tikki was bounding all round Nagaina, keeping just out of reach of her stroke, his little eyes like hot coals. Nagaina gathered herself together, and flung out at him. Rikki-tikki jumped up and backward. Again and again and again she struck, and each time her head came with a whack on the matting of the veranda, and she gathered herself together like a watch-spring. Then Rikki-tikki danced in a circle to get behind her, and Nagaina spun round to keep her head to his head, so that the rustle of her tail on the matting sounded like dry leaves blown along by the wind.

He had forgotten the egg. It still lay on the veranda, and Nagaina came nearer and nearer to it, till at last, while Rikki-tikki was drawing breath, she caught it in her mouth, turned to the veranda steps, and flew like an arrow down the path, with Rikki-tikki behind her. When the cobra runs for her life, she goes like a whip-lash flicked across a horse's neck.

Rikki-tikki knew that he must catch her, or all the trouble would begin again. She headed straight for the long grass by the thorn-bush, and as he was running Rikki-tikki heard Darzee still singing his foolish little song of triumph. But Darzee's wife was wiser. She flew off her nest as Nagaina came along, and flapped her wings about Nagaina's head. If Darzee had helped they might have turned her; but Nagaina only lowered her hood and went on. Still, the instant's delay brought Rikki-tikki up to her, and as she plunged into the rat-hole where she and Nag used to live, his little white teeth were clenched on her tail, and he went down with her – and very few mongooses, however wise and old they may be, care to follow a cobra into its hole. It was dark in the hole; and Rikki-tikki never knew when it might open out and give Nagaina room to turn and strike at him. He held on savagely, and struck out his feet to act as brakes on the dark slope of the hot, moist earth.

Then the grass by the mouth of the hole stopped waving, and Darzee said: 'It is all over with Rikki-tikki! We must sing his death-song. Valiant Rikki-tikki is dead! For Nagaina will surely kill him underground.'

So he sang a very mournful song that he made up on the spur of the minute, and just as he got to the most touching part the grass quivered again, and Rikki-tikki, covered with dirt, dragged himself out of the hole leg by leg, licking his whiskers. Darzee stopped with a little shout. Rikki-tikki shook some of the dust out of his fur and sneezed. 'It is all over,' he said. 'The widow will never come out again.' And the red ants that live between the grass-stems heard him, and began to troop down one after another to see if he had spoken the truth.

Rikki-tikki curled himself up in the grass and slept where he was – slept and slept till it was late in the afternoon, for he had done a hard day's work.

'Now,' he said, when he awoke, 'I will go back to the house. Tell the Coppersmith, Darzee, and he will tell the garden that Nagaina is dead.'

The Coppersmith is a bird who makes a noise exactly like the beating of a little hammer on a copper pot; and the reason he is always making it is because he is the town-crier to every Indian garden, and tells all the news to everybody who cares to listen. As Rikki-tikki went up the path, he heard his 'attention' notes like a tinny dinner-gong; and then the steady 'Ding-dong-tock! Nag is dead – dong! Nagaina is dead! Ding-dong-tock!'

That set all the birds in the garden singing, and the frogs croaking; for Nag and Nagaina used to eat frogs as well as little birds.

When Rikki got to the house, Teddy and Teddy's mother (she still looked very white, for she had been fainting) and Teddy's father came out and almost cried over him; and that night he ate all that was given him till he could eat no more, and went to bed on Teddy's shoulder, where Teddy's mother saw him when she came to look late at night.

'He saved our lives and Teddy's life,' she said to her husband. 'Just think, he saved all our lives!'

Rikki–tikki woke up with a jump, for all the mongooses are light sleepers.

'Oh, it's you,' said he. 'What are you bothering for? All the cobras are dead; and if they weren't, I'm here.'

Rikki–tikki had a right to be proud of himself; but he did not grow too proud, and he kept that garden as a mongoose should keep it, with tooth and jump and spring and bite, till never a cobra dared show its head inside the walls.

This story is by Rudyard Kipling.

A SELECTED LIST OF TITLES
AVAILABLE FROM CORGI BOOKS

THE PRICES SHOWN BELOW WERE CORRECT AT THE TIME OF
GOING TO PRESS. HOWEVER TRANSWORLD PUBLISHERS
RESERVE THE RIGHT TO SHOW NEW RETAIL PRICES ON COVERS
WHICH MAY DIFFER FROM THOSE PREVIOUSLY ADVERTISED IN
THE TEXT OR ELSEWHERE.

All Corgi Books are available at your bookshop or newsagent, or can be ordered
from the following address:
Transworld Publishers Ltd,
Cash Sales Department,
PO Box 11, Falmouth, Cornwall TR10 9EN

Please send a cheque or postal order (no currency) and allow £1.00 for postage and
packing for one book, an additional 50p for a second book, and an additional 30p for
each subsequent book ordered to a maximum charge of £3.00 if ordering seven or
more books.

Overseas customers, including Eire, please allow £2.00 for postage and packing for
the first book, an additional £1.00 for a second book, and an additional 50p for each
subsequent title ordered.

NAME (Block Letters) ....

ADDRESS ....

....